The PIZZA
THAT TIME FORGOT

to Amber Hudson

Matt DeAndrea

RUMBLE!

Other Avon Camelot Books by
William L. DeAndrea and Matthew DeAndrea

WHEN DINOSAURS RULED THE BASEMENT
NIGHT OF THE LIVING YOGURT

The PIZZA
THAT TIME FORGOT

William L. DeAndrea and Matthew DeAndrea

AN AVON CAMELOT BOOK

AVON BOOKS, INC.
1350 Avenue of the Americas
New York, New York 10019

Copyright © 1999 by William L. DeAndrea and Matthew DeAndrea
Published by arrangement with the authors
Visit our website at **http://www.AvonBooks.com**
Library of Congress Catalog Card Number: 98-93055
ISBN: 0-380-79155-2

First Avon Camelot Printing: January 1999

CAMELOT TRADEMARK REG. U.S. PAT. OFF. AND IN OTHER COUNTRIES, MARCA REGISTRADA, HECHO EN U.S.A.

Printed in the U.S.A.

OPM   10   9   8   7   6   5   4   3   2   1

To My Dad
William L. DeAndrea
1952–1996
I Miss You.

If it weren't for the fact that we'd be going back to school in about a week and a half, it would have been an ideal afternoon. The weather was warm, but not hot, we had some great food to eat, a bunch of old books to explore, and a tree house to lie around in.

That had been the deal. The three of us (Gemma Davis, my best friend; Michael Parlo, my genius younger brother; and I, Jonathan Parlo) had spent the morning cleaning out the attic of Gemma's house. Gemma's dad's family had lived there since the 1920's when the house was built, and over the years, they had accumulated some neat stuff—toys, games, adventure books, and big heavy flat phonograph records of weird sizes, with different kinds of holes in them. I don't think I'd ever known anyone who had the kind of machine it would take to play them.

Mr. Davis had grown up to be a science fiction writer.

I don't know if growing up in that house, with the kind of people who accumulated that kind of stuff had had anything to do with it, but I wouldn't be surprised if it had.

Anyway, the tree house was a lot younger than the house itself. Gemma's mom had built it in the beginning of the summer. She'd had minimal help from Gemma and me, and Michael fetched and carried as well as he could. Michael is seven, and Gemma and I are twelve, so we did what we could.

Gemma's mom didn't need much help, anyway. She owns a store downtown, typewriter, computer, and copier sales and repairs (she met Mr. Davis when he came in to copy his manuscripts) and she's really good at building and fixing anything.

And so she built the tree house.

Actually, it's a platform about nine feet off the ground that bends around the tree like big pieces of pie. In the middle, there's a trapdoor strong enough to stand or sit on, and a double railing all around the outside.

She built a nifty metal ladder into the side of the tree, and gave us an incredible length of knotted rope. You could rig a basket to it and haul things up, or it could be used as an emergency exit. So there we were, up in the tree house. We'd hauled up some books and other things from the attic. The stuff was faded a little with age, but was otherwise in great shape.

The book I was reading, for instance—it was called *Don Sturdy Captured By Head Hunters* by Victor Appleton, all about a kid who gets stranded on a jungle island and chased by everything scary known to kids in 1924—didn't smell at all like an old book, and the pages didn't flake when you turned them.

Gemma, in the meantime, was making soft, tinkly music, like music from a music box, only muffled.

"That's nice," Michael said. "What is it?"

Gemma held it up for him to see. It was a box made of unvarnished wood, a little bigger and fatter than a videocassette with a hole cut in the top, and little prongs of metal screwed into the wood so they'd stick out over the hole.

"Says on it it's an African thumb harp," she said. "You pluck the prongs with your thumbs and—"

She brought the music back.

"How can you play it already? You've never seen one like it before, have you?"

"No," she said, "but it's simple. A lot easier than a guitar."

"Oh," I said. "Of course."

Gemma played guitar, piano and flute. So far. And now, African thumb harp. I probably couldn't make a guitar go *twang* if I dropped it out a window.

Michael had something I knew something about—a stereopticon. I'd seen one in the museum at the state university when Mom took us there one day. It had a little scope and a wooden slide with a handle. A bunch of double photographs (black-and-white) mounted on cardboard went into the slide, and you adjusted it until you got a 3-D image. The neat thing about it was that a lot of the pictures were about real news of the day. Michael, for instance, was looking at pictures of the Spanish-American War, which took place more than twenty years before the house was built—but you get the idea. History is *my* department, if you can say I have one.

I told Michael I would like to see that sometime later, and he said sure and asked if he could read my books.

Now, when I said before that Michael was a genius, I meant it. He has special science stuff to study that this big professor at Princeton University sends to him, and he does it, usually within three days of the time the envelope gets to our house.

Right now, in fact, as he looked at the stereopticon, he was already muttering stuff like "Focal length should be proportional . . . mmm hmmm . . . curvature of the eyeball can be ignored . . ."

I don't even know if he knows he does it.

But for all of that, he's still a seven-year-old kid. There's nothing about dinosaurs he doesn't know (okay, not so unusual—but he knows it in *Latin*), but he also scares himself to death on those rare occasions when he gets to see *The X-Files*.

Michael loves *Indiana Jones* and *The Three Stooges* and . . . and . . . he's a seven-year-old kid, that's all.

But the book, the slides, and the thumb harp had been put away now, because Gemma's mother had raised lunch for us in the basket. We had a Sicilian pizza from Tino's plus an orange and a couple of sodas each.

Cleaning out the attic had been fun, but it had also made us hungry. And thirsty. So for the next few minutes the noises were mostly chewing and gulping. It was a lot more noise, I've got to admit, than there would have been if we'd been sitting at a table with grown-ups, but what's the sense of being a kid if you can't act like kids when you're alone together?

After awhile, the hunger didn't cut so badly, so we did some talking as well. I looked up at the sky through the trees, enjoying the chewiness of the pizza and the

4

sting of soda bubbles on my throat, and I kind of sighed and said, "This is so great."

Gemma giggled, wrinkling her freckled nose. "My mother must really have wanted that attic straightened out. She's waiting on us now like everyone did that time my Dad was the guest of honor at the science-fiction convention."

"She knows we'll have to come down soon," Michael said.

There was a bit of a tremble in his voice. That wasn't good.

Michael had a specialized fear of heights. He's got no trouble going up the tree. He's got no trouble being *in* the tree. It's coming down that's the problem, and, believe me, it can be a *huge* problem. At the beginning of the summer, Gemma and I once spent an hour and a half trying to get my brother to go down that ladder, trying to explain that with the soft grass underneath, and the tree house less than ten feet up, even if he did fall, the chances of his being hurt were tiny.

That actually didn't make much sense on our parts, because as far as I can tell the whole thing about a phobia is that it doesn't *make* sense. It wasn't a matter of being hurt. It was a matter of falling, plain and simple.

It was probably the maddest I've ever been with him (Gemma was much more patient), which was totally unfair, because in the first place, almost everybody's scared of something. With me, it's dancing. The idea of moving around to music holding a girl (or even a broomstick, for crying out loud) and making it *look good* at the same time absolutely petrifies me. So I don't go to places where I might be forced to dance. Except relatives' weddings, in which case I limp and say I hurt my knee at football practice. Even in the summer.

In the second place, it was really unfair to Michael to be so mad because I used to have the same kind of trouble.

What I also had was a dad, who somehow knew the right combination of humor, sympathy, and exasperation that helped me get over the problem.

Dad died when Michael was two years old. Mom is the greatest—she keeps her busy law firm going while still finding plenty of time for Michael and me. But she's never been a boy, and I'm *only* a boy. I don't remember the right words. Sometimes Michael suffers for it.

Well, I thought, Michael's been a lot better about it recently. Maybe today it wouldn't be much of a problem to get him down. In the meantime, I figured we had another good hour and a half before we actually had to worry about getting home and meeting Mom.

She was in the State capital, arguing a big school bus safety law in front of the Legislature. There was a good chance she'd be on the news that night. We were so proud of her we could bust.

I sat back on a cushion, took a big, chewy bite of pizza, and a swig of my still-cold soda.

Then the tree started to grow.

2

Well, no. The tree had started to grow years and years ago. Now, though, it was growing *fast*. Like a mushroom. Like a time-lapse film of a dandelion blooming.

Like an elevator going up, with us in it.

It started to sway, too, even as we could see the ground pulling away from us.

"Out of here *now*," I said.

I don't know why I bothered. Gemma was already doing the right thing and had gone a few steps down the ladder. She had also grabbed hold of one of Michael's arms and was encouraging him toward the trapdoor.

That was something we had agreed early on never to do, but Gemma and Michael and I had been through enough emergencies to recognize one when we saw one.

"All right, all right," Michael said to her. "I'm phobic, not stupid! Let me take a breath."

He did, a good deep one, and then he went down the hole while he let it out.

There's the answer, I thought. All we had to do was make the tree act bewitched, and we could get him out of it.

Now I realized *I* needed to snap out of it. There was already going to be a bit of a jump at the bottom of the ladder. Time for me to get moving, too, but not before I made sure the knotted rope was tied on tight and tossed it over the side.

Then I went down.

I don't know how much higher we were now than we'd been when we started out, but I ran out of ladder a *long, long way* before I ran out of tree.

That didn't make any sense, either. Trees grow from the *top*. They don't come squeezing out of the ground like some kind of solid toothpaste.

The branch I was in was twenty feet off the ground and getting farther off the ground every second. I didn't have nearly enough ladder.

I grabbed for the rope. It was out of reach. It was only a few inches out of reach, but it might as well have been in Canada.

In a few seconds, I was going to be a mangled heap at the bottom of this tree.

Then the rope came swinging toward me. I was so startled, I missed it, but I got it the second time.

The genius was saving my life. Standing on his tip-toes, Michael had grabbed the bottom of the rope and swung it toward me.

I caught hold of it just in time. If I'd missed it again, Michael wouldn't have been able to reach it again. I didn't waste a fraction of a second getting down that rope. When I got to the bottom of it, I still had about a six-foot drop to the ground.

I dropped gladly. I lay there on the ground, catching my breath, and watching the tree zoom up into the clouds like Jack's beanstalk.

Gemma was coming over to see if I was all right. Michael was already there.

"Yeah, I'm fi—" I started to say.

Just then, something wet, warm, and gushy came flopping out of the sky and splattered on my thigh.

"Yaaaaghhhh!" I screamed, wiping frantically to get it off me. I grabbed a wad of the stuff from my skin and threw it into the grass.

Gemma walked to it and flipped it over with a twig. She looked at it for a few seconds.

"Pizza," she said.

Michael gasped. "Our pizza!"

Naturally. We seemed to be going through the start of another strange, earth-threatening adventure, and he was worried about the food.

"Michael," I said, as another piece flopped to the ground and one last can of soda left a fizzy trail through the sky. "I think that's the least of our worries."

"What do you mean?" Gemma said.

I pointed up into the tree.

"Well," she said. "The tree's stopped growin—"

She never did get out that last *g*. It's hard to talk with your jaw dropped open.

"It's not even the same tree," she said.

"I thought so," I said. "Michael?"

I didn't look around for him. I didn't figure he'd gone far and I couldn't take my eyes off the tree.

"Michael?" I repeated. "What kind of a tree is that?"

Michael seemed pretty distracted himself. He turned briefly to look at the tree.

"It's a maple," he said.

I was willing to take his word for it. I could tell a dandelion from regular grass, but that was about it.

I wasn't done with him yet.

"What kind of tree did we climb?" I asked him.

"Jon, gee. It was an oak. Oaks make acorns. Maples make the little helicopter things."

Of course, he knew the scientific name for the helicopter things (he probably knew the scientific name for acorns, too) but he was humoring his dumb brother, something he hardly ever does.

I was about to get mad at him, but I realized that if I did, it would only be because I was scared, and that was the same reason he snapped at me.

And he was *very* scared. I could hear it in his voice when he spoke again.

"Guys, please forget about the trees for a second and look over here. Please?"

We looked, but we didn't see anything.

That was the point. *We didn't see anything.*

"The house is gone," Gemma said, very matter-of-fact. Then: *"MY HOUSE IS GONE!"*

She didn't mean it was destroyed. A pile of rubble would have been bad enough to find, but at least it would have been something.

We didn't find any rubble. We didn't find—anything. Not a stick, or at least not a stick that didn't have bark on it. It was as if Gemma's house had never existed.

Gemma ran out into the middle of the grass and

weeds and ferns and twigs where the house she'd lived in all her life had been until just a few minutes ago.

She was sobbing and screaming. "Mom! Mom! Where *are* you?" Then after a while, she switched it to, "Where am *I?*"

She turned to Michael and me. "The *Twisters* did this, didn't they? Didn't they? What did they do to us this time? Where *are* we?"

Now, I better stop here and tell you something. Gemma Davis is no helpless damsel in distress. I don't care how tough you think you are. If you almost get killed, lose your house and your mother practically before your eyes, and see all the laws of nature abolished in the space of ten minutes, you're going to be scared and scared good.

Gemma was reacting now, getting kind of hysterical. She'd get over it in a few minutes.

After that, she'd be fine. Better than fine. She'd be the most clearheaded and bravest of all of us.

Well, certainly braver than I was likely to be. I've learned a lot of guy stuff about not showing your feelings, especially the "weak" ones. But just because you don't show them doesn't mean you don't feel them. However this thing turned out, I knew from experience that I'd be a lump of Jell-O inside until it was over. I'm not going to dwell on it or anything. I just want you to know.

Michael was already taking the best first step toward getting Gemma back to normal. He was ignoring the hysteria and simply answering her questions.

"Well, in the first place, it's the Twisters who did this."

(I'll tell you all about the Twisters pretty soon. I

admit I've been putting it off because I don't even like to think about them.)

"Of course it's the Twisters," Michael said. "Who else has the technology to pull this stuff off? Who else would *want* to?"

"I hate them," Gemma said.

"I'm not fond of them myself," I said.

Gemma laughed and rubbed some tears from her cheek. I knew she was going to be all right.

"As for *where* we are," Michael was going on, "you've got to give the final answer on that, but I think we're where we always were."

"What do you mean?" Gemma said. "My house isn't here. It's been there since 1920. Where did it go?"

"Take a look around."

"Michael," I said. "Come off it, huh?"

Gemma made a chopping motion with her hand and shushed me. She was looking *and* listening, so I did, too. Gemma started to move through some of the brush, following a sound, the rush of water around stones. Just like I thought, the noise was made by the brook that ran through the Davis property.

I followed. I saw it at the same time she did—the rock bridge.

It wasn't a bridge that anyone had built. It was a formation of big, flat, whitish slabs of rock that had fallen, or been pushed by a flood, in such a way that they arched a little over the water. You could cross it easily and never get your sneakers damp.

The genius had done it again.

"I thought everything looked the same around here. Except that there was no house, of course."

"Or anything else either," I said.

12

This time, it was their turn to ask what I meant.

"It just occurred to me," I said. "Look, just past us is where the house is supposed to be. Then what? The flowering hedges you've got out there."

"Those are forsythia bushes," Gemma told me.

"Not anymore, they're not. Bright yellow like that, we couldn't miss them. Past that, there should be the Methodist Church, and just past that should be Route Six."

I looked at my watch. "About twenty after one. There should be traffic on Route Six right now. A lot of it."

"Yeah," Gemma conceded. "And it's not there. They wiped out the whole town. They finally figured out how to do it."

Michael looked dubious.

"I don't know," he said. "It would be an awful big technological jump for the Twisters, considering the state we left them in last time."

"No, Gem," I said. "I don't think so."

"Don't think what?"

"That they wiped out the whole town."

"Why not?" she asked.

Michael grunted. "Why are we still here?"

Gemma frowned. "Maybe they only wiped out the stuff on the ground, and we were in the tree and too high up—that wouldn't work. Why is the tree still here?"

Michael rubbed his chin and opened his eyes wide, respectfully.

"Right. That's really good. I hadn't even thought of anything like that. I was thinking that the Twisters are planning to use Marsdentown as a jumping-off spot to take over the whole *planet*. They're not going to bother holding a grudge against us. Heck, I bet they can't even tell us from any other human kids.''

''Hey, we've messed up two of their big plans.'' Gemma seemed offended that the Twisters wouldn't remember us after that.

''They've done some terrible stuff to us,'' I pointed out. ''And threatened to do worse, and I couldn't tell two Twisters apart if you paid me.''

That was true. Unless they were standing right next to each other, they looked identical. Their tree-bark-like skin varies from gray to dark brown, verging on black.

Gemma sighed. ''I guess you're right.''

I was just about to tell her how that was the *good* news when my genius brother, Mr. Diplomacy, piped up.

''Gemma,'' he said. ''When we first went through this you were yelling for your mom. Where's your dad?''

Gemma's face started to cloud up again, and who could blame her? I wondered if strangling Michael would make her feel better.

I grabbed him by the shoulders and hissed at him, *''What's the matter with you? Aren't things bad enough—''*

Michael squirmed under my hands and looked confused.

''What's wrong?'' he demanded. ''I was just going to tell her there was nothing to worry about as far as her parents are concerned.''

Gemma was smiling. ''He's right. Let the twerp go.''

I let him go.

''I just forgot for a second,'' Gemma said. ''Dad's up in Millerton. There's a big new mall. This giant bookstore is having a grand opening, and Dad is signing books all day."

"See?" Michael said. "Boy, Jon, you've got to give me some credit sometimes, okay?"

"Okay, slugger. I'll do my best. So I'll start by letting you take your best shot at figuring out what's happening to us."

That was no big deal, actually. It was pretty much the way we always did it. I heard of a football coach who explained using his star player all the time by saying, "When you have a big gun, you shoot it."

Michael's brain was our big gun.

"I don't think there's any question that we've gone through another time warp. Not to the Jurassic Period like the last time, but at least before 1920."

"Why then?"

"Gemma's house was built in 1920."

"Sure," Gemma said. "And it's not only my house. There's no neighborhood at all. Also we went back to a time when a big old maple stood in the spot where our oak tree was. Is. Will be. Whatever."

"We know what you mean," I reassured her. "The question is, how far back?"

"Mmm," Michael said. "That sure is the question."

"Look," Gemma said. "A thousand years in the past isn't going to help us much more than a million years would."

"I don't think it's a thousand years," I said. "I don't think the rock bridge or something like that is likely to last a thousand years."

They supposed I was right.

"Now it's your turn," Gemma said.

"What are you," I asked. "The referee?"

She grinned and ruffled her carroty hair. "Exactly. What should we do now?"

"We should head west, toward town. To see if there is a town. We're going to have to find a place to sleep, even if it's only a doorway. And maybe we'll find some answers."

"Well," Gemma said, "we'll probably at least get better questions. Let's go."

"Not yet," I said. "Let's check around the base of the tree and see what else came through with us." We had learned it was a good idea to get all the facts we could, no matter how unimportant they seemed.

"And hope the first thing we run into isn't a bear," Michael said.

It wasn't a bear. As we got back to the tree, the first thing we saw was a Twister.

It was using a single tentacle to stuff the last of our pizza into the ugly mouth hole on top of its head.

3

It wasn't an ordinary Twister.

There was nothing unusual about the way it was built—it had the peculiar shape we had come to hate and fear.

It was built like a thick palm tree, with the trunk split a little more than halfway up into four branches—except that they weren't branches at all. They were tentacles. The tentacles were flexible and incredibly strong. I know. I've struggled against them. At the ends of the branches were frond-like things the Twisters could use like fingers.

Tucked between each pair of tentacles, making four in all, were bright green globs, like unripe grapefruit or huge limes. We called these their eyes, but we weren't sure.

The skin (or bark) varied in color from Twister to Twister, but not that much. It seemed to be smooth, but it had to have openings in it, because Twisters were capable of reaching into it from time to time, the way you'd reach into a small pocket, and pulling out little gadgets that they used to work their machinery.

At the very top of them, between the tentacles, was an X shape, the kind the Boy Scout manual tells you to make over a snakebite before you suck out the poison. This was the mouth—at least, it was what they used for eating. And boy, could they eat. This thing was taking each big, thick slice of Sicilian pizza and swallowing it whole in a quarter of a second. When all the pieces were gone, it turned around and looked for more. It paid no attention to us. Then, I guess because there was no more pizza, it shuffled off into the woods.

Twisters split again at their bottoms into four more tentacles, shorter and less flexible, but a lot stiffer and stronger. That's what they move on, hopping and twisting, which is why we called them Twisters.

Michael started to chase after this one, but Gemma and I each grabbed him by a shoulder and almost pulled him down onto his butt.

"Easy, squirt," Gemma said. "He may have friends."

"Good point," Michael said. We stood there and watched the Twister disappear into a stand of trees.

"He probably does have friends," Michael said. "He's kind of a runt, isn't he?"

"Look who's talking," Gemma said.

"Ha," Michael said. "I'm seven years old. I've been getting bigger my whole life. I don't expect to stop till I get taller than everybody. But have we ever seen a Twister who was less than maybe eight feet tall?"

"A lot taller with their tentacles up," I conceded. "You're right, little brother."

"Of course I'm right," Michael said.

"Don't push it," I warned him. "This guy we just saw couldn't have been much more than four-and-a-half feet tall."

"Do you suppose," Gemma mused, "that this could be a *baby* Twister? Do they have babies?"

"I don't know," I said. "That didn't come up in the conversation that we had with Slarn that time."

Hold it. Time-out. I'd better stop and explain some things before I get so far behind that I'll never be able to do it. So as well as I can, I'm going to tell you who the Twisters are, and what they want.

A long time ago, in a galaxy far, far away . . .

I know. I know. I can't help it.

Anyhow, back then and out there, there was a civilization that was already ancient. They had used up their natural resources and polluted their planet, and only a strict and ruthless dictatorship that rationed everything from food to living space managed to keep things going at a level of misery.

Then there arose a group of Twisters who couldn't stand to live that way. They considered mounting a revolution, but even if they won it would only mean that they'd be in charge of the mess their planet had become.

So they decided to try to escape. Twisters didn't have rocket ships. They couldn't spare the metal or the fuel.

What they did know about was vibrations. Not just the kind of stuff that makes music when you pluck a string, but the basic kind, the secrets-of-the-Universe kind. The kind that draws the line between what matter is and what energy is. The kind that governs Space and Time.

Michael knows a lot more about this. In fact, what you're getting now is what I managed to understand from his three solid days of trying to explain it to me.

Turns out, there are at least five universes kept apart by these specific vibrations. And just like towns on a map, there are points where they almost touch. It so happens that the best touching spot for all five universes—the Crossroads of Creation, if you want to call it that—happens to fall exactly where Horatio Marsden set up a little town in 1808.

Marsdentown is a great town. Good climate, good schools (so my mother says), low crime, friendly people. I don't know any kids who'd want to live anywhere else.

Can we help it if the place turned out to be a landing strip for monsters? Sometimes, I thought of it as Monstertown instead of Marsdentown.

Actually, it was the landing strip for monsters long before old Horatio put down roots.

Remember when I said, "A long, long time ago . . ."?

I wasn't kidding. When the Twisters first landed on earth, the primary inhabitants were dinosaurs, specifically late-Jurassic dinosaurs.

Gemma and Michael and I, when we first found this out, wondered about it. Here they were, the only intelligent life the planet had ever seen. Why didn't they just take over? They'd have a mostly empty planet. They could keep humans from ever developing. There's their happy ending.

But they couldn't. These were beings that had what we'd call super-science, but they couldn't build a rocket ship. It wasn't just the lack of resources on their own planet. It was the technology they had developed, and the technology they *hadn't* developed. They couldn't build a city or a truck either. They had no idea how to find metal or get enough of it out of ore—or how to make anything out of it once they did get it out.

So they used their vibrations to scope the future, and they found the perfect time for them to invade and take over.

Our time. The late 1990s. Here's why.

There were all kinds of basic machines, up and running. Lots and lots of stone and metal and other things were already dug up and ready to use. There wouldn't be too much in the way of opposition from us, because we hadn't developed enough to deal with their invasion technologies. We already worry about pollution and crowding (nobody's saying we shouldn't), but by the Twisters' standards, this is still an empty planet.

All they have to do is kill off a few billion humans, and it's all there.

And maybe they couldn't build a truck, but one thing a dictatorship always figures out how to do is kill people.

They had war machines. They had this thing that could be tuned to the human nervous system and kill us dead in our tracks, without harming any other kind of animal.

Their problem was that they needed *time* to set these things up. Time travel was one of the most difficult things they did, and they needed to get their war machines through the warp and powered up again before they could get going. They needed at least forty-eight hours uninterrupted in Marsdentown before they could take on the earth.

So the first part of their plan was to kill everyone in town, or scare them out, during the vulnerable time.

They originally thought they would open a time warp in the middle of town and send through some hungry allosauruses. Before they were ready, an accidental stray vibration caused a small warp to appear in Michael's and my basement. We got trapped in the past (which was when we learned most of this stuff), but we managed to escape back to our own time, wrecking as much as we could of the progress they'd managed to make so far.

Their second attempt was to send a deadly bacteria (one of its side effects was to turn a blob of gallons of yogurt into a thinking monster), but we were ready for them that time, and we thwarted that plan, too.

So we had saved the earth. Twice. If you want to send us a medal, that would be great, but a better thing you could do is figure out some way to get people to believe us. The only grown-up I'm even able to talk to about this stuff is Gemma's dad, and he treats it all like a science-fiction story. He laughs and says what great imaginations we've got.

It's very hard, feeling responsible for the safety of the entire world. Too much pressure for three kids. It gets to the point where we'd *like* to think we made it all up, somehow, like we hypnotized each other into believing it.

Then something like this happens.

Something that is happening to the three of us, and it's happening right now.

Whenever ''now'' is.

And we have to deal with it. Which we do, as well as we can manage.

After some discussion—You want to go in the same direction as the Twister? No, even short they scare me to death. But how else are we ever going to learn anything?—we decided to follow our original plan.

We searched the area around the tree. We found a couple of soda cans and some sticky patches on the grass and dirt where soda had spilled and begun to dry. And we found the thumb harp. Gemma picked it up and brought it along.

"You never know," she said.

"You sure don't," Michael said.

We set off through what used to be Gemma's neighbors' backyards (and houses, come to think of it), looking for a town that might or might not be there.

4

I don't suppose we would have noticed much out of the ordinary in the woods during that walk if we hadn't been looking. But we were on the alert, and we saw things. Mostly things that seemed to have been torn off trees, cut or bitten with some kind of four-bladed thing, then tossed aside.

"Exactly the sort of mark you'd expect a Twister mouth to leave," Gemma observed.

"Taste-testing," Michael said. "This is one hungry Twister. Maybe he's little because he's malnourished."

I didn't know. If you could concentrate on working out the little parts of a problem, you could not only hold back from panicking on what to do about the big problem, you might even be putting the pieces together to get the big problem solved later on.

It really works, and not just for fighting alien invaders. It was something my Dad told me that I *do* remember.

A little farther along, we saw something else in the almost-path we were walking along. It was about six inches long, fluffy, and gray. It looked like a big furry worm.

"Now what?" I asked nobody in particular.

Michael, being practical as usual, had picked up a twig—Gemma had told him to make darned sure it was a twig—and was advancing on it to check it out.

It didn't move when he poked it with the stick. It simply flipped over, showing more fur, with a little blood at the skinnier end.

"Squirrel tail," Michael said. "It caught a squirrel and liked it."

"Uuuug!" Gemma said. I couldn't blame her. The idea of dangling a wriggling squirrel over your mouth, then chomping him off at the base of the tail was a little gross for me, too. But Gemma seemed to get right over it. "I wonder why it didn't eat the tail?" she said.

"I don't know," I said. I could play that way, too. "Too much hair and not enough meat, I guess."

Michael just shrugged and flipped the tail into the woods, and we moved on. If we'd known that in about three minutes we'd run into something a million times grosser than a severed squirrel tail, we might have sat with it for hours.

The first thing that got us was the smell.

This was not the kind of bad smell you get most of the time, something horrible in the air you have to walk through. This was one of those special stinks, a brick wall kind of smell. It's something horrible in the air you walk through with a hard smack that almost floors you. It gets into your nose and your mouth and your eyes, and for a second or two makes you unable to talk or even to move.

We actually had to turn our backs on it, it was so bad. It didn't help too much to do that, but it let us talk a little.

"Geez," I said, "What is it?"

"It's bad," Gemma informed me.

I wiped tears from my eyes. "Thank you so much. Very helpful."

"My mission in life," she said.

Michael, being who and what he is, was trying hard to answer the question.

"Something is rotting," he said. "I think we'd better fight our way through this and find out what it is."

Gemma and I said it simultaneously. "Are you nuts?"

"Look, I don't like it any better than you guys do. But does it smell like anything on earth?"

"No."

"Does it smell like anything you can *imagine* on earth?"

"No," we admitted glumly.

"Then I think for our own safety, we'd better find out what that smell is."

Gemma nodded but she didn't like it. "Right again, squirt," she sighed.

Michael had said the magic words. For most kids they're "please" and "thank you," but we've passed beyond all that. Or sunk below it. Our magic words were, "For our own safety."

So we held our noses, or picked flowers to sniff, which did about as much good as holding a newspaper over your head in the middle of a typhoon, and followed the smell.

You didn't have to be a bloodhound to do it, either. About seventy-five yards away, around a bend in the trail, there was a big steaming mound of greenish-red muck that spread across the trail from one side clear to the other.

It was a Twister. The first dead Twister we had ever seen.

"Look at it," I said.

"Do we *have* to?" Gemma asked.

It was decaying so fast, steam coming off it made it hard to see details.

Michael tried to wave some away with his hand, but this was no more useful than nose-holding or flower-sniffing. "No wonder their hides are so tough—their insides can't stand what's in the air outside."

"You mean if they get cut open, they die?" Gemma demanded.

"On earth, anyway. It's a pretty sure guess," Michael said. "They've probably evolved to withstand the air on their home planet.

"But this is great," Gemma said.

"How?" I asked.

"They can die. We can kill them. And if we can kill them, we can *beat* them."

"Of course we can beat them," I said. "They know we can beat them. Why do you think it's so important for them to get everybody out of Marsdentown before they build their war machines? If we could just get the grown-ups to believe us—"

"If," Michael said.

"Well," Gemma said. "I don't care. I hadn't thought

27

of it before, and it makes me feel a lot better. We'll win the grown-ups over somehow.''

And you know, I was starting to believe her. Of all the kids I've ever known, Gemma Davis is easily the best at dealing with adults.

Michael pointed at the ground. "There's proof right there," he said. "All we have to do is take home a chunk of that guy—"

I became aware of the full smell of our dead friend again and said, "Do *you* want to carry a piece of that around until we find a way home?"

Michael's little-boy nose wrinkled up.

"Now that you mention it, no," he said. He took another look. "Won't do us any good, anyway. He's rotting away before our eyes. There won't be anything left but slime in fifteen minutes."

"Do me a favor," I requested. "Don't say *slime.*"

He grinned at me. "Okay, big bro."

I turned my attention back to what was left of the body. I speculated that he might have run into a bear.

"Nah," Gemma said. Gemma goes on nature walks with her mother, and she's always saying she's *seen things* in the woods. "A bear doesn't slash as long or as straight as this—right down the middle, from arm branches to foot branches. The bear's claws would veer off there somewhere. And a bear's claws are much sharper than whatever got this thing. They'd have a cleaner edge. This looks ragged, almost as if it were torn instead of cut."

Michael's eyes lit up in the way they do when he thinks of something so neat, he even impresses himself.

"It *was* torn," he said with certainty. "Only it was torn from the *inside.*"

28

"The inside?" I echoed.

"Yep. They're some kind of animal-vegetable hybrid, isn't that what we decided before?"

We conceded that. At least, it was the best guess we had, and the only one that fit all the facts we knew for sure.

"All right," Michael said. "Well, the Twisters have to reproduce somehow. I mean, we saw the baby. So let's say they reproduce like hybrids. They bud, like some plants do, and the baby Twister grows in the bud, in the—the—abdomen. Or whatever it is. And then when it's big enough, it splits off."

"And when the little one splits off, there's a time when the big one has some of its insides exposed to the air," Gemma jumped in.

Michael nodded at us happily. He loves it when we get it.

"It makes sense. Remember the first time we met them, one of them said they were born with the knowledge and memories of their parent. Budding could explain that."

"It also means," I said, "that they have immunity from the germs or whatever on their own planet, or they'd die every time they reproduced. They wouldn't have any population growth on the planet at all. There's not even anything they can do about it—or can they? I mean, do they just reproduce and it's out of their control, like plants?"

"I don't think it matters," Michael said. "We've got the new one to deal with. He may be little. But he's healthy. And he's *starving*."

We looked again at the unhealthy one. It was hard to believe, but the smell was practically gone. So was the body. There was just—what I'd asked Michael not to say.

Time to press on. None of us wanted to step in it, so we took some extra time and made a little loop off the trail around the tree.

I kept it to myself at the moment, but I was certainly encouraged by that little trail in the woods. It wasn't much, but it was there, just wide enough for people to pass on it. Somebody—somebody *human*—had made that trail, and even if it had been Native Americans who were still a thousand years from seeing their first white person, the sight of a human face was something almost too beautiful to imagine.

But we didn't see any humans, Native Americans or otherwise.

What we saw was the mass of what looked like a moving tree.

Our little Twister friend.

5

The three of us did what we wanted to do this time, with unanimous consent, no conference needed. We ran like crazy. A glance back over my shoulder showed that the Twister was thinking the same way, and running away from *us*.

I don't think I mentioned before that Twisters can "run." Of course, just as they don't walk as we do, they don't run the way we do, either.

And they don't run in the twisty way they walk, either.

To run, they throw themselves lengthwise on the ground and thrash their long limbs in a combination swim and crawl.

We'd only seen them do this once or twice, outdoors. It looks very clumsy, but I don't suppose there's a lot of room on their home planet to practice. They thrash up a lot of dirt and leaves as they go. They make a lot of noise, too.

But they cover a lot of territory in a short time. If the little one had been trying to catch us, he would have done it by now.

Especially since Michael and I stopped running to watch Gemma pause to do what we figured was the dumbest thing we'd ever seen her do.

She was playing her grandfather's thumb harp. Something that sounded vaguely African, but I don't know anything about music. She told us later it was a simple four-note progression that her "fingers just found" on the instrument.

Whatever it was, the Twister loved it. It dragged itself upright and came toward us in its usual slow Twister walk.

"Why is it doing this?" I asked.

Michael sighed. "Vibrations. The Twisters do everything with vibrations. Don't you remember? Sound is vibrations. Music is vibrations. These vibrations must sound good to it. Or maybe just *interesting*."

Gemma kept playing, and the thing kept coming. It was as if they were both hypnotized by it.

Michael broke the spell.

"When it gets here," he demanded, "what are we supposed to do, dance with it? You're the only one who can play that thing."

Gemma started to laugh and dropped the harp in one hand to her side.

Down the trail, the Twister stopped, too.

I froze, getting ready to yell a warning to run if the Twister should take it into his brain (wherever it kept it) to chase us after all.

But it didn't. It just stood there looking at us. Or at least it stood there with two of its bright green lime-looking things pointed in our direction. Then it seemed to shrug its tentacles and ambled off on the angle from the trail it had been on when it had started to run.

We were happy to let it go. We gave it a few minutes, then resumed the trail ourselves. My only worry, which I kept to myself, was that this would give the Twister a shot and an angle from which to ambush us. I didn't say anything about it because it didn't seem to want to ambush us.

The sun was getting lower in the sky and we still had to find a place to eat and sleep, if possible. Due east, following the sun and the trail, was our best way of finding a town, if there was any town to find.

". . . and I just wanted to see if we could make a vibration that reached them in any way at all. I wasn't being stupid," Gemma insisted. "I was gathering facts for the future."

Michael shrugged. "Not stupid. You just scared me to death."

Gemma grinned. "Me, too, when the Twister actually started heading for us—"

"Why didn't you stop playing then?" I asked.

"I don't know," she said, and I could see that she was confused herself. "I was scared and fascinated at the same time. You know, the way rabbits are supposed to be fascinated by snakes, except they aren't really. But I'm glad you made me stop, Michael."

"You're welcome," Michael said automatically. "The thing of it now is—"

We never did find out what the thing of it now was, because a loud noise cut through the woods like a buzz saw.

It was a voice, a human voice, and ordinarily we

would not have considered it pleasant. Right now, it was one of the most beautiful sounds imaginable.

"Hey there! Hey! What the devil are you boys doing on my property?"

6

I shushed Michael and Gemma, not because I was scared this time but because I wanted to hear the sound of English, even gruff, angry English. I'd been so scared that the only three voices I would ever hear again would be our own.

Then it came.

"That's right! You! You kids! This property has been posted. I could shoot you and be within my rights."

"Okay, mister," I said. Instinctively, I raised my arms as my companions did the same. "Please don't shoot. We're kind of lost."

"Okay, okay," he said. "Just step out to the middle of the trail so's I can get a better look at you."

Hands still up, we edged sideways into the trail. That's when the man saw Michael for the first time.

"Aha. Three of you. Never hurts to be too careful. All right, all right, put your arms down."

We put our arms down. Gemma was breathing right into my ear. It sounded like she was breathing through a microphone. Michael had put a hand on my leg and started to squeeze. He was squeezing hard enough to hurt.

I was trying to figure out where we were—in time. The man we were looking at was wearing old-fashioned clothes, but they weren't *that* old-fashioned. The rifle he was carrying wasn't that old-fashioned, either, just kind of awkward-looking.

"All right now," the man said. "My name's Bernard Charlton and I own all the land out here past the creek. All of it. Got it handed down to me from my grandfather."

"Yes, sir," I said.

Gemma and Michael didn't say anything.

"I don't know any of you," Bernard Charlton said. "You don't come from around here. Do they know what trespassing is, where you come from?"

"Yes, sir," I said again. I would have dropped the "sir" if Bernard Charlton had dropped the rifle, but he didn't seem interested.

"That's right," Bernard Charlton said. "This is my property, and everything on my property I own, no matter what it is. Do you get that?"

"Yes, sir," I said again.

Michael tugged at my leg. "No," he hissed. "He can't own us. He can't."

Bernard Charlton looked a little confused. "I've got a gold mine on this property. And it's mine. No matter what she says, the old witch. It's mine."

"Who's she?" Gemma asked into my ear.

"I've got the missing link," Bernard Charlton said

proudly. "I've seen it. And if it's on my property, I mean to have it. Dead or alive."

Michael exploded. That's one of the problems with being a boy genius. You think everybody else knows everything you know, but they're pretending not to.

"The *missing link,*" Michael demanded, hopping from one leg to the other. "The *missing link?* There is no missing link. Are you crazy? Nobody believes in the missing link anymore."

"That just means you're ignorant," Bernard Charlton said with satisfaction. "There was a man over in England, Charles Darwin, died some time ago now, he's the one found out about the missing link. Man was descended from the monkeys and we just have to find the animal that came right between, the missing link—"

"I know what Darwin says," Michael said hotly, "and he doesn't say that man is descended from the monkeys. And I know what Gould says, too, and Richard Dawkins. There's been a lot of research since Darwin. Nobody talks about missing links anymore. We've *got* all the links. The way evolution works—"

"Michael," Gemma said, grabbing him by the shoulder. "Michael, shush."

"Wait a minute," Bernard Charlton said.

His face had gone pasty-white. I turned around and looked behind us. I thought there had to be a Twister back there. Bernard Charlton looked horrified.

"Wait a minute," he said again. Then he advanced on the three of us, rifle waving in the air, looking scary enough to make us think we ought to run. At the last minute, though, he dropped the rifle. Then his hands shot out and he grabbed Gemma by the shoulders.

"What's your name?" he demanded, looking deep into Gemma's eyes.

Gemma squirmed. "Gemma Davis," she said, her voice sounding high and squeaky. Gemma never sounds high and squeaky. She could sound calm in the lap of a grizzly bear.

Bernard Charlton dropped his hands to his sides. "Lord in heaven," he said. He bent to pick up the rifle. "Lord in heaven, it's a girl. Half-naked. It's a girl."

"I'm not half-naked," Gemma said. "I'm wearing shorts."

"You're all half-naked," Bernard Charlton said, "but for the boys, it doesn't matter. But a girl."

"Look," Gemma said, starting to explain.

"It's the time warp," I said, interrupting her. I knew this was useless. Nobody ever believes us when we try to tell them this stuff. For Gemma's sake, I thought I had to try. "I don't know what year this is," I said, "but we came from the year 1999 and in that year, girls and boys dress pretty much the same and also they dress like we're dressed now so you see—"

"I'll take you back to the house," Bernard Charlton said. "No, that won't be any good. I know what I'll do. I'll take you to Doverby, that old fraud. He'll have to believe me now."

"Who's Doverby?" I asked. I knew it was too much to hope for a town scientist, but I hoped anyway. I figure that if we go on fighting the Twisters the way we have been, we're going to have to have some halfway decent luck every once in a while.

"Doverby's the chief of police," Bernard Charlton said. "Truth to tell, he's the only police. He just likes to sound important."

"Right," I said.

"He'll know what to do with you. And then he can go out and arrest that old bat for sending trespassers onto my property. You did say 1999."

"1999," I repeated.

Bernard Charlton pointed the gun at us again. I really didn't like it when he did that.

"Go that way," he said. "Just keep on walking till we get to the carriage. And don't forget. I caught you trespassing on my property. I could shoot you dead if I wanted to and be well within my rights."

"We really didn't mean to trespass on your property," I said.

"Wait a minute," Bernard Charlton said. He let his rifle drop to the floor again. Any one of us could have picked it up and shot it at him. In any one of the cop shows I like to watch back home, that's exactly what the hero would have done. None of us did it.

Bernard Charlton took off his jacket and handed it to Gemma.

"Put that on," he demanded. "You don't look decent the way you are. You can't go parading through town in nothing but that. That old witch ought to be arrested, making you dress like that." He leaned over and picked up his rifle. "Okay now, all of you. Let's go."

Michael went when the rest of us did, but he wasn't happy about it.

"The missing link," he kept saying under his breath. "The missing link. For Pete's sake."

7

Gemma looked funny in Bernard Charlton's jacket—like she was dressing up for Halloween—but she trudged along in it without complaining. Maybe having a rifle waving around to the back of her made her as nervous as it made me. Maybe she just couldn't believe she wouldn't be able to get around this grown-up the way she had all the other grown-ups in her life.

"So," she said. "This missing link. How do you know that's what it was?"

"I know," Bernard Charlton said. "I can read. I get *The Scientific American.*"

"Well," Gemma said. "That's good, you know, but well—what did it look like?"

"It looked like a man, half of it," Bernard Charlton said. "It looked like half an ape, too. That's the point."

I could feel that Michael was on the verge of exploding again. I put out my hand and grabbed him by the shoulder and squeezed hard. Michael winced.

"What do you expect it to look like?" Bernard Charlton demanded.

"Oh, I don't know," Gemma said. "Maybe I thought it would look like a tree."

"Trees are plants," Bernard Charlton said. "Lord in heaven, you children are ignorant. Didn't you ever get any schooling at all?"

"There's a road," Michael said, pointing to a dirt patch up ahead of us.

There was a carriage, too. It was low-slung and black and hitched to a single, forlorn-looking horse. The horse seemed to be asleep on his feet.

"The old bat doesn't believe in the missing link," Bernard Charlton said. "Doverby doesn't, either. But I'll show them. I'll show them. I'll have my picture in *The Scientific American* with the missing link sitting right in my lap, dead or alive."

Michael tugged at my arm and nodded toward the thick stand of trees to our right. It took me a moment to see it, but I did: a full-size black gorilla, silky and huge. It was holding a last, bedraggled piece of pizza and nibbling at the tip. I nearly jumped into the air.

Michael grabbed my arm and shook his head at me. He was right. We couldn't tell Bernard Charlton about the gorilla. He would have shot it.

I just wished I knew where it had come from.

Right about then, we all got to the carriage. Bernard Charlton waved his rifle at it and said, "Get in, get in," so we did. We had to climb up on this rickety wooden step to make it.

The horse started off down the dirt road. The carriage

bounced and rattled. It was a good thing we hadn't had a chance to finish the pizza. Everything in my stomach was being churned into—well, never mind.

After what seemed like forever, the road suddenly became paved, sort of. It wasn't asphalt, the way I was used to, but cobblestones and binder.

"Look," Michael said suddenly, pointing ahead of us. "It's the Methodist church."

He was right. It was the Marsdentown Methodist Church, the one we were used to. When we had seen it this morning, though, it had had a big wooden cow out in front of it, announcing the getting-to-know-you barbecue the church held every summer. There was no cow out in front of it now.

"Look," Michael said again, pointing in the other direction.

Now I was looking up the hill, and it was a hill I recognized. The Civil War Memorial was sitting in the middle of the little square. City Hall was right where it was supposed to be, at the square's far end. We were on Marsdentown's Main Street, and everything was where it belonged, but—

"Look at the War Memorial," Gemma said. "You can read the date. M-D-C-C-C-X-C-I. 1891."

"Look at *that*," Michael said.

That was the little stretch of storefronts at the edge of the town square. This morning, they'd been fronted by plate-glass windows. Now they had small square ones. The door closest to us had a big sign on its door saying that William Jennings Bryan was coming to speak in Canterbury, two towns away.

"William Jennings Bryan," I said.

"Won't get anywhere," Bernard Charlton said. "Liv-

ing in the past, that's what that man is. Governor Mc-
Kinley will take care of him.''

"McKinley was elected president,'' Gemma said. ''I
remember that.''

Bernard Charlton didn't seem to hear her. He had
taken the horse and carriage around the square. Now he
came to a stop directly in front of City Hall. He dropped
the reins and jumped out.

"Here we are,'' he said. ''You all get out now. This
is where the police are, and this is where you're going.''

"You mean we're going to get arrested for trespassing?'' Michael asked him.

Bernard Charlton was about to answer, but he didn't
have a chance. He was holding out his hand to help
Gemma down from the carriage when the front doors
of City Hall burst open and a woman came rushing
out—except that at first, I didn't realize it was a woman.
She was that fast and that strange. She appeared in a
whirlwind of feathers and lace. Every piece of clothing
she had on her was black.

"You,'' she said, pointing a quivering finger at Bernard Charlton. ''You tool of the forces of evil and this
earth, I have put a stop to you.''

"Me!'' Bernard Charlton exclaimed. He dropped
Gemma's hand in midair. Gemma stumbled to the
ground and had to pick herself up.

"You set these children on my property,'' Bernard
Charlton shouted. ''You're too much of a coward to
come looking yourself, you old witch—''

"The spirits of the dead are with me,'' the woman
said. ''The spirits of the dead can see into your lies and
your deceptions and your scheming and they will avenge
themselves—''

43

"You old bat," Bernard Charlton said.

I was glad Bernard Charlton had left his rifle in his carriage. If he'd had it, he probably would have used it. Instead, he rushed at the woman in black with his arms out, meaning to do I don't know what.

Just then, the doors to City Hall opened again and a tall, heavyset man came out. Big as he was, he was fast. He got Bernard Charlton by the arms before I really had a chance to see him move.

He picked Bernard up and moved him aside.

Then he crossed his arms over his chest and said, "All right, you two. I've had enough."

8

This was the place where a twentieth-century cop would have pulled a gun, but Chief Doverby didn't have a gun. What he had was a temper, and it was barely under control.

"Listen, you two," he said, ignoring Michael, Gemma, and me. "I've had enough trouble for one day. I don't need anymore."

"You wouldn't have so much trouble if you weren't such a small-minded man," the lady in the feathers sniffed. "And so ridiculous, thinking I would go out and steal some man's chickens."

"She stole chickens?" Bernard Charlton said.

"That's *enough*," Chief Doverby said. "Harriet, I want you to go right home and stay there—"

"I'm going to go to court against that man," Harriet said. "That's slander, what he said about me. Stealing his chickens as if I needed chickens—"

"You are a chicken," Bernard Charlton said. "You have the brain of a chicken—"

"I'll bring you to court, too," Harriet said. "I'll bring this entire town to court. I'll take my story to the New York newspapers."

"You'll take your story to your own front parlor," Chief Doverby said. "And you'll keep it there, too, until I'm ready to hear from you again. And if you don't, Harriet, I give my oath I'll lock you up for disturbing the peace."

"You should have locked her up for trespassing," Bernard Charlton said.

"I'll lock you up with her," Chief Doverby said. "Don't think I won't. Just because you're the richest man in town doesn't mean you can get away with anything you want—"

"Look what she did here," Bernard Charlton demanded. "Look at these three. She sent these three out on my property to steal the missing link."

"There is no such thing as the missing link," Michael said furiously.

Chief Doverby suddenly turned his attention to us. Actually, he turned it to Michael, nodded at the boy genius approvingly.

"That's right," he said. "I've been trying to tell Mr. Charlton over here just that for months now. That man Darwin over in England, he was some kind of crank."

Michael's mouth dropped open in shock and snapped shut. Chief Doverby came right up to him and looked him over.

"Bernard, what's the matter with you?" he asked.

"The boy's hardly wearing any clothes. None of them are hardly wearing any clothes."

"I'm not the one that's kept them out of clothes," Bernard Charlton said. "It was Mrs. Winthorpe here that did that. Sending them over to my property to steal the missing link—"

"I never sent anybody anywhere," Mrs. Winthorpe said. "I don't traffic in children. I commune with the spirits—"

"You commit fraud in your front parlor three nights a week," Chief Doverby said, "and don't think I don't know it. Are you responsible for these boys being dressed like this?"

"I've never seen any of these boys before in my life."

"Bernard?"

"They were on my property," Bernard shouted, hopping mad.

"You sure you didn't haul them out there yourself?" Chief Doverby asked.

"What would I do that for?"

"Well," Chief Doverby said, "maybe you were looking to buy yourself a few witnesses. So that the rest of us would buy the story about you seeing the missing link."

"He'd do anything at all to make himself look important," Harriet Winthorpe said.

"Old fraud," Bernard Charlton said.

Chief Doverby turned back to us. "What about you boys?" he asked. "You have an explanation for why you're running around half-naked?"

"We didn't think of ourselves as being half-naked," Michael said. "This is what we wear around home."

"And where's home?" Chief Doverby asked.

Michael looked at his shoes. Gemma and I looked at each other. The part of town where our houses would stand was now Bernard Charlton's big vacant field. I knew we couldn't say we lived there.

Michael looked up from his shoes and said, "I'm not sure exactly where we live. It's a long way off, I think."

"Lost," Chief Doverby said sagely.

Michael looked at his shoes again.

Chief Doverby sighed.

"I'm going home," Bernard Charlton said. "If you aren't going to arrest anybody. But I'm warning you. That thing is on my property, and I mean to have it for myself. It's going to make me famous."

Bernard Charlton turned on his heel and stomped off.

"That's an evil, evil man," Harriet Winthorpe said righteously. "I know. The spirits have told me."

"Go home," Chief Doverby said.

He turned his back on her—and that's when I saw it, sticking out of the back pocket of his coat. It must have been there all along, but with all the commotion, it hadn't registered on my brain.

"Chief?" I got his attention away from Michael. "Is that today's newspaper? Could I see it for a minute?"

"See the newspaper?"

"Yes, sir. That's right."

"Can you read, boy?"

I suppose it wasn't a stupid question, but it rankled anyway. I nodded. The chief reached into his pocket and got the newspaper out. I thanked him for it and unfolded it to the front page. I let my eyes go straight to the date.

August 16, 1899.

We were a hundred years out of time. We were away from the warp. We were being held captive by a lot of perfectly nice people who wanted to change our taste in clothes.

Chief Doverby had a horse-drawn buggy, too. It wasn't as fancy as Bernard Charlton's, but it was bigger. He also had a deputy. The deputy was sitting at the only desk in the police department office, looking hot enough to melt. Everything looked hot enough to melt, and I felt hotter. I looked around the "department's" single room and decided it wasn't a department at all, but I didn't know what to call it.

The deputy stood up when Chief Doverby came in. He looked us over as if we had just crawled out from under a pile of particularly nasty rocks and sniffed. The chief went striding over to this big armoire kind of thing and opened the doors.

"Clady?" he said to the deputy. "Didn't we have a bunch of horse blankets in here?"

Horse blankets, I thought. In this heat?

Clady scraped long fingers across his head. "Tom

Barden says you said you'd stop out to his place for lunch. I told him it wasn't on your way to anywhere, but he wasn't paying attention.''

"I'll stop over," the Chief said.

"It was dogs got those chickens," Clady said. "You know it as well as I do. Harriet Winthorpe never put any spell on Tom Barden's trees. And if she had, it wouldn't have took.''

Gemma and Michael and I looked at each other quickly. A spell on the trees. I didn't like the sound of that.

Gemma and I both sidled over to Michael. When we were close enough, we bent our heads together and started to whisper.

"What is it with this Mrs. Winthorpe?" I asked. "It's a little late in history for her to be a witch, isn't it?"

"Theosophy," Gemma said. "It's kind of like channeling. It was really big in New England and New York State around the turn of the century. Except that instead of channeling three-thousand-year-old pharaohs, they channeled dead relatives and people like that.''

"Stupid," Michael said. "And I bet they charged money, too.''

"Of course they charged money," Gemma said. "Channelers charge money. Mrs. Winthorpe is probably making her living getting people to think she's talking to the dead.''

"Look," I said. "I think the point here is this business about the spell on the trees. Do either of you have a better explanation of a haunted tree than an active Twister?"

"No," Michael said.

"Found 'em," Chief Doverby said. He had emerged

from the armoire carrying a huge pile of the thickest wool blankets I had ever seen. They would have been too much for me in the middle of February.

The chief marched over to us and handed out the blankets.

"Put these around your shoulders," he said. "That'll keep you decent until I can get you home to my wife."

Gemma wrapped one of the blankets around her and winced.

"It's scratchy," she said.

The chief looked at her curiously. The blanket covered almost her entire body. He couldn't see much of anything but her eyes and the top of her head.

"They're scratchy but they're all I've got," he said finally. "You kids ready to go?"

"Yes, sir," Michael said.

Chief Doverby marched us back into the sunshine where his buggy was waiting. The blanket I was wearing was not only scratchy, but also heavy. I was sweating so much my clothes were soaking wet.

Michael climbed into the buggy and hunkered down, coming as close to looking as if he wanted to cry as I'd ever seen him. Michael's so smart, I sometimes forget he's only seven.

Chief Doverby pulled the buggy out onto the road. Gemma hung out the side of the carriage and looked at the scenery as if she'd never seen it before.

"We'll get you three boys home to Mrs. Doverby," the chief said, "and that'll take care of everything."

"Just as long as she doesn't play with Ouija boards and dress like a bat," Gemma said under her breath.

"We'll just stop out at Tom Barden's place and try to convince him nobody put a spell on his trees," the chief said. "Not that you can convince Tom Barden of anything. Ignorant old fool."

Michael put a hand on my arm and tugged. "Look," he hissed into my ear.

I looked—down the length of the dirt road that would one day become Route 6, down into the trees that would one day be cleared away so that the houses we lived in could be built. It took me a while to understand what Michael was getting at because I was making the opposite of the old mistake. I wasn't seeing the trees for the forest.

Michael grabbed my chin in his hands and practically forced my head in the right direction.

"Look," he hissed again.

Chief Doverby didn't hear him, because Chief Doverby was talking to himself, mostly about Tom Barden and his haunted trees.

I, in the meantime, was seeing one of those haunted trees. It was tucked away in the middle of a lot of ordinary trees, but there was no mistaking it for anything but what it was. There's something about a Twister that's as sinister as the sound of heavy breathing coming from behind you in the dark.

This Twister was standing still, but its tentacle-branches were snapping and coiling and reaching out into the leaves around it.

I could tell it was getting itchy.

10

We should have done something about it right away. We wanted to do something about it right away—or at least I did—but too much was getting in the way. Chief Doverby had stopped the carriage next to what looked at first like just more vacant land. The Twister was right up in back of it, at the start of a little ridge. The chief jumped down from the carriage and began walking along a well-worn dirt path that led to a low, sagging-roofed house with a wide arc of packed dirt around it. It was the kind of place that would have given the Marsdentown Zoning Board a full-scale temper tantrum in 1999. It was tiny. The walls and roof looked like they were about to collapse. I was willing to bet anything it didn't have an indoor bathroom.

I looked over at Gemma and Michael. They both nodded. We all climbed out of the carriage and onto the ground.

"He didn't tell us we couldn't come," Michael said.

Gemma gave him a withering look. We all knew that didn't mean anything when it came to grown-ups. I made a mental note to be better about that kind of thing when I was a grown-up. I think all kids make mental notes like that, and then forget them as soon as they get older.

"Did you see the Twister?" Michael asked Gemma.

Gemma looked in the direction Michael was pointing. She took a sharp breath and winced. "What's it doing there? Why is it so quiet?"

"I think it's waiting," I said.

"For what?"

"I don't like it just sitting there," Michael said. "Twisters don't just sit there. They attack."

I was going to tell him that we didn't know what Twisters did, really—we'd had a lot of experience with them, but we hadn't exactly made a scientific study of their habits—when the Twister began to move. It didn't move forward or backward, which would have been easy to spot, and easy to understand. It started turning around and around on its base. Then its tentacle-branches began to move up and down, as if it were doing jumping jacks.

"It looks like Mom when she does that workout tape," Michael said.

The Twister stopped jumping and walked out a little into what must have been Tom Barden's property. It was stretching its tentacles into the open area of the lawn, keeping them low to the ground, reaching farther and farther until—

"What is that?" Gemma said, as the tentacle snapped

back toward the trees carrying a writing mass of blood-red feathers.

"It's a chicken," Michael said, sounding sick.

We all looked at one another at once. We were all thinking the same thing. This time, somebody besides us had to have seen it. Chief Doverby and Tom Barden were right down there at Tom Barden's house, much closer to the Twister than we were. They must have been looking right at it.

"Come on," Michael said urgently, beginning to run down the hill.

Gemma went after him without a second thought. I looked back at the Twister, just in case. All we needed to do was run right into the arms of a Twister attack.

The Twister had blended back into the trees. If you hadn't been looking for it, you wouldn't have known it was there.

I hesitated one more moment. Looking at all that open space did not give me a good feeling. If Chief Doverby and Tom Barden had seen the Twister grab that chicken, shouldn't they be running out to look at it?

I started down the hill, much more slowly than Gemma and Michael had gone. I caught sight of them, standing to the side of the house when I'd only gone halfway down the slope. Michael was looking at his feet again. Gemma was holding the blanket around her shoulders and looking ready to cry. Chief Doverby and Tom Barden were pacing back and forth in the dirt, scratching their heads.

"They didn't see it," Gemma said.

"How could they not have seen it?" I demanded.

"They were looking at the scratches on the ground," Michael said reasonably.

"Sometimes I think we're all going crazy," Gemma said.

Michael gave her the kind of patient look that is going to end up getting him in trouble someday. It was definitely not the kind of look women like to see from men when they're upset.

I sidled over to Chief Doverby and Tom Barden and looked at the scratches on the ground. They were Twister tracks, all right. I would have known them anywhere.

Michael came up behind me. "Baby," he said.

"I was thinking the same thing. They're small tracks. I don't see any bigger ones, do you?"

Michael shook his head. "I think the bigger ones just sit out there and wait. Or they're being careful. Maybe the little one doesn't know any better."

Tom Barden was still tromping back and forth in the dirt, obliterating tracks with every step. "She made these tracks herself," he was saying, "all because I told the truth that she's a fraud and a cheat and you know it. Stupid old cow—"

Chief Doverby sighed. "Do these look like Harriet Winthorpe's footprints to you? Do they look like *anybody's* footprints?"

"She's trying to confuse us," Tom Barden said. "You know she doesn't talk to spirits with that Ouija board of hers."

"But what would she want with your chickens?"

"Revenge," Tom Barden said grimly.

Chief Doverby shook his head. "I'd as soon think it was Bernard Charlton's missing link. That would make as much sense. Got to be some kind of animal been getting in here, though."

"Whatever it is, I'm going to get it," Tom Barden said. "I'm going to get it if I have to sit up all night with a rifle."

"You're going to end up shooting yourself in the foot. Get a little sense. Pen the chickens in, Tom."

Tom Barden's face went purple. It was as if the chief had suggested hanging underwear instead of a flag from the town flagpole. "You don't pen chickens," he said. "What are you thinking of?"

"I'm thinking you ought to get yourself another wife, if you can find a woman who will have you. You're going strange living off by yourself. It's some kind of animal did this, Tom, and I don't want to hear any more about it. Pen the chickens so they can't get got at. That's all I can tell you."

"It's because she's rich, that's the reason," Tom Barden said. "Got that big house left to her. Been cheating the public in it ever since."

Chief Doverby turned to us. He didn't look surprised to see us, and he didn't look angry, either.

"Back in the buggy," he said. "Let's get on out to my place. It wouldn't happen to be any of the three of you that was stealing chickens, would it?"

I looked down at the tracks in the dirt. "I wouldn't know how to make tracks like that if my life depended on it," I said.

"Neither would I," Chief Doverby said. "Let's get going, then. See you later, Tom. Try to stay peaceful."

Tom didn't answer. Michael and Gemma and I followed Chief Doverby up the hill, back to the buggy. Chief Doverby was muttering under his breath the whole time. I didn't blame him.

When we got all the way up the hill to where we had started, I turned around and looked back at the trees.

The Twister was still there, big and ugly, but it wasn't moving anymore.

Maybe it had gone to sleep.

11

It was Mrs. Doverby who discovered that Gemma was a girl. Bernard Charlton had discovered it, too, but he hadn't told the chief, and the chief hadn't noticed. Considering the way Mrs. Doverby carried on when she *did* notice, I was grateful that Gemma had gone so long undetected. You'd have thought we'd presented Mrs. Doverby with an ax murderer, complete with weapon.

"Oh, my heavens," Mrs. Doverby kept saying, running in circles around Gemma and throwing her hands in the air. "Oh, my heavens. What could your mother have been thinking?"

Mrs. Doverby was a big, soft-looking woman. She suited her husband and her house so well, it made me think of Christmas stories about Mr. and Mrs. Claus.

"Oh, my heavens," Mrs. Doverby said again.

Gemma raised her eyes to the ceiling of the big front porch. The Doverby house was huge, much bigger than anything a police chief could afford in 1999. The porch alone was bigger than the living room in Michael's and my house, or Gemma's. Then there was the big front tower, round as a ball, with a little peaked roof on it. I wracked my brains, trying to think of a house in Marsdentown in 1999 that might be this one, but I couldn't come up with anything.

Doverby was sitting down on a wicker porch glider.

"What were you thinking of?" Mrs. Doverby demanded of him. "Letting a young girl like this roam around town worse than naked with a lot of boys and men—"

"She wasn't worse than naked, Margaret," Doverby said. "She had that blanket over her. And I didn't know she was a girl. How was I supposed to know? Look at that hair."

We all looked at Gemma's hair. It looked the way it always looked.

"I thought," Chief Doverby said, "that you could fix them up with some clothes and some food and all that kind of thing. And that once we got them calmed down a little, maybe we could straighten out a few things—"

"Where are their parents?" Margaret Doverby demanded.

"Don't know as they have any," Chief Doverby said. "And they're lost. And they had Bernard Charlton waving his rifle in their faces and then we ran into Harriet Winthorpe and then somebody's stealing Tom Barden's chickens or a fox is getting to them, except you know what Tom's like so—"

Margaret Doverby gave her husband an exasperated look and marched over to the front door. It was a doubledoor arrangement, actually, with stained glass instead of

61

solid wood on the panels. The frame around the glass was carved into curlicues and waves. I was used to all the straight lines and easy-to-clean surfaces of modern houses. I thought this was great.

Margaret Doverby stuck her head through her front door and called out. "Trudy! Jack! Come down to the porch, please!"

I moved closer to Michael. I couldn't move closer to Gemma because Mrs. Doverby had her by the wrist and was dragging her around the porch whenever she moved herself.

"Trudy and Jack must be the kids," I said.

"I wonder how old they are," Michael said. "If they're practically grown up, they aren't going to be any help."

"Right," I said. "But maybe we'll get lucky. Maybe one of them will be a big fan of science fiction."

"In 1899?"

"They had science fiction in 1899. Jules Verne. H.G. Wells."

"Yeah, well. This is *our* luck we're talking about. So you try to explain it to them."

"I will," I said.

Michael can be surprisingly naive about people, but he can also be surprisingly cynical. I guess it's hard on a seven-year-old kid never to meet anybody who can keep up with him in brainpower. I can't even keep up with him in imagination.

There was a thundering in the house, and then a tall boy came running through the front doors. Michael's face fell. This boy looked young enough in some ways—his face was almost as naive and innocent-looking as Michael's own—but there was no mistaking the muscle development or the height. Jack Doverby had to be at least sixteen. And sixteen was old enough so that we might not be able to get him to believe us.

A moment later, the front doors opened again and a girl came out, tall and thin, with dark brown hair braided across the top of her head and tied back at the nape of her neck. Michael brightened immediately. This girl was no older than Gemma.

"I like her," Michael whispered to me. "She's going to be smart. Just you watch."

I liked her, too. She was carrying a book in her hands, a copy of something called *Elsie Dinsmore* by Mrs. Eden Southworth.

Jack Doverby had walked over to Gemma and was staring into her face. "Oh, my gosh," he said. "Look. It's a girl. It's a girl and she's—"

"Never mind what she is," Margaret Doverby said. "There's two boys to attend to as well. You get right upstairs this minute, Jack Doverby, and take these two with you."

"Jon," I said, as politely as I could. "Jon Parlo."

"You take Jon and this other one with you—"

"Michael Parlo," Michael said.

"—and get them some proper clothes. And Trudy and I will take this one—"

"Gemma Davis," Gemma said.

Jack Doverby goggled. "You mean she's walking around looking like that with two boys who aren't even her own brothers?"

Trudy Doverby raised her eyes to the ceiling of the porch and then lowered them. Then she caught Gemma's strained glance. The two of them smiled at each other, almost. Their lips twitched and their eyes crinkled. They didn't let it go any further than that. I saw it, but neither Jack Doverby nor his mother did.

Mrs. Doverby was all bustling efficiency. "Let's go now," she said. "I will not have children badly dressed and unfed in my house."

12

If I'd had a choice, I would have skipped the costume change and gone right for the food. It felt like hours since we had all been sitting up in the tree house, eating a perfectly decent pizza. I looked at my wrist. I was wearing my dad's watch, one of the few possessions of his I have. Usually, I leave it off and in my room, where I know it will be safe. My dad didn't leave a lot of stuff behind when he died. He wasn't the kind of person who had a lot of stuff. The last thing I wanted was to get into some kind of trouble where I would lose or break that watch.

Jack had a big room at the front of the house, with high ceilings and a curved window with a window seat that looked out over his front lawn. I tried one more time to think of where this house could be in Marsdentown in 1999, but I came up blank. It was making me a little crazy. Marsdentown isn't that big a place.

Jack dressed Michael up first. While I was checking out the window seat and wondering just where we were in town, Michael was getting stuffed into knickers, white stockings and a white shirt with an enormous Peter Pan collar.

"You got to put this on," Jack said.

I turned to look and saw Michael all togged out, with his arms crossed over his chest and his face set in the most mulish expression I had ever seen it wear. Jack was holding something black and long and stringy.

"I am not going to put that on," Michael said savagely, "and if you think you can make me, you've got a surprise coming. I'm not as much of a wimp as I look."

"What is that?" I asked.

"It's a bow," Jack said. "You put the bow on under the collar and it hangs—I mean, everybody wears them."

"Not where I come from, they don't," Michael said.

"Where do you come from?" Jack asked. "Don't you come from the United States?"

"I come from 1999," Michael said grandly, "where nobody wears knickers and bow ties and nobody talks about missing links. You ought to try this stuff on, Jon. Just you wait. You can hardly move."

"You must have been talking to Mr. Charlton," Jack said. "He's the one who says he's seen the missing link. My dad says there isn't any such thing. It's just something missing in Mr. Charlton's head."

"If we're dressed up like this," Michael said, "we aren't going to catch the Twisters or anything else, because we aren't going to be able to move. How are we going to run all trussed up like this—"

The next sound we heard was a low-throated wail. It was followed by the crash of wood on wood, as if a chair had fallen over—or been thrown. Jack was on his feet in an instant.

"That's Trudy," he said. "There's something wrong with Trudy."

He rushed out of the room, and we followed him. The hall was as high-ceilinged as his bedroom. It was also dark and twisty and hard to see in. Jack raced down a corridor and we went on following him. Michael was limping a little, as if his clothes hurt him even more than he said.

Jack got to a door and knocked loudly—but by then I would have known where we were going anyway. There hadn't been any more crashes, but the wailing had really gotten into gear, and I could tell it was Gemma's voice.

"*Oh,*" she said. "This is *impossible.* How can you *stand* this stuff? This is *awful.*"

Jack knocked again, just as Michael and I came down behind him. The door to Trudy's room opened slightly and Trudy poked her head out.

"We're not ready yet," she said.

Gemma came up behind her and pushed the door all the way open. Then she marched out into the hall.

"Look at this," she said. "I can hardly breathe in this thing. And run? How am I going to run?"

Gemma was dressed in a bright-yellow dress that went almost all the way to the floor, but that wasn't the half of it. She also had on what seemed like a million petticoats. Her sleeves were puffed and high on her arms. Her legs were encased in the same kind of white stockings Michael had on, except they were longer.

"It isn't ladylike for a girl to run," Jack said haughtily.

Gemma ignored him. "I'm wearing at least *four* sets of underwear," she told me. "It's ridiculous. And everything binds. And there's so much of it. How do these people put up with this?"

Trudy Doverby bit her lip. "Oh, dear," she said. "Isn't this the kind of thing they wear where you're from? This is all anybody ever wears around here. And in New York, too. My mother gets the fashion magazines . . ."

"You shouldn't talk about underwear in front of boys," Jack said. "That isn't ladylike, either."

"Oh, Jack," Trudy said. "For goodness' sake. Maybe Gemma just comes from someplace where they've done something sensible about women's clothes—"

Jack turned to me. "Bloomers," he said. "That's the kind of thing my sister approves of these days. *Bloomers.*"

"What are bloomers?" Michael asked.

Gemma stalked back into Trudy's bedroom and sat down on the edge of the bed. We all trailed in after her. Trudy's bedroom was full of books, the way Jack's was full of sports equipment. All the books seemed to be by women writers I had never heard of.

"We've got to do something about this," Gemma said. "We can't have me bound up like this forever. I'll be useless. And what about the Twisters?"

"I think you only have to stay dressed like that until we find a way back through the warp," I said. "There is a way, remember. We've done it before."

"I know, I know," she said. "But at this rate, I may never get to the warp. Jon, I'm not kidding. It's impossible to move in these clothes."

"So what *do* they wear where you come from?" Jack asked, exasperated.

"They wear what I was wearing when I got here," Gemma bit out. "Shorts. And T-shirts. And—"

"You were practically naked when you got here!" Jack shouted.

"No, I wasn't," Gemma said. "I was wearing what everybody I've ever known wears in the summer and I want it back. Oh, I can't believe this—"

"They did look comfortable, those things you were wearing," Trudy said musingly. "It's true about these clothes. They do bind."

"There isn't anyplace where people wear clothes like that," Jack said. "You just name the place. You just name it."

Gemma hopped off the bed and advanced on him. "1999," she proclaimed. "Do you get that, you idiot? This is 1899 and we come from 1999 and we came through a time warp and I wish we could go back right this minute."

"1999?" Jack said. "You can't come from 1999. People can't go back and forth in time. It doesn't happen."

"It happened to us," Gemma said.

"Prove it," Jack said.

Jack was practically shouting by that time. I had no idea how we were going to "prove" that we came from a hundred years in the future. I was sure someone would be pounding up the stairs any moment, trying to find out what the commotion was about. I wouldn't have minded telling everybody that we came from 1999, but I didn't want to get everybody mad at us in the meantime.

I had just about given up hope—I thought Gemma

was going to brain Jack Doverby with one of Trudy's books—when Michael came up with his most brilliant idea of the afternoon.

"I know how we can prove it," he said, in that high, clear, little-kid voice of his. "Jon, show them Daddy's watch."

13

This is the thing about my father's watch. It's not just a watch, it's an entire solar system tracking device. Michael's and my dad may not have collected a lot of stuff, but when he did, this is the kind of stuff he collected. My mother has a cigarette lighter on the night table in her bedroom that's a green metal replica of Godzilla. Dad bought it in New York City when the movie *Godzilla 1985* came out, even though he never smoked a cigarette in his life. The watch is that kind of thing, although I think it was more expensive. It's digital, and if you press one of the tiny buttons on its rim, you get all kinds of information. You can even get the face to change into a picture of the solar system that moves, with the planets both orbiting and revolving. I asked my Mom once where Dad had bought it, but she didn't know. He'd had it before they'd ever met.

I took the watch off my wrist and handed it to Jack.

Trudy crowded in next to him so that she could look at it, too.

"Look," Trudy said. "It doesn't have hands. It just has numbers. And they—beat, sort of, like a heart."

Jack shook the watch and held it to his ear. "It doesn't tick," he said. "How can it tell time if it doesn't tick?"

"It's got a microchip in it," Michael said.

"A microchip is this little piece of plastic with electronic wiring on it," I said, and then I gave it up. I don't really understand that kind of stuff myself, and if Michael tried to explain it, nobody would understand it. I leaned forward and pressed one of the tiny buttons on the watch rim. The solar system came into view.

"Oh," Trudy said.

"There are too many planets," Jack said. "There are—"

"Those were discovered later," Michael said. "Would you pay attention to us? For Pete's sake."

Trudy sat down on the bed. She had a dreamy expression on her face, as if she'd just discovered the Holy Grail.

"1999," she said. She turned shyly to Gemma. "Do women have the vote in 1999?"

"Don't be crazy," Jack said. "Women aren't ever going to get the vote. Women aren't smart enough to understand politics."

Gemma had a wicked gleam in her eye. If we hadn't needed Jack's help, as well as Trudy's and everybody else's, in fighting the Twisters, I wouldn't have given two cents for Jack's chances of survival.

"Gemma," I warned.

"Don't get in my way," Gemma said.

"We've got the Twisters to fight. Now. We don't have time—"

"Can I at least tell her that women got the vote in 1920?"

"You just did," I said.

"And that's not the half of it," Gemma said.

I was about ready to stuff her head in a pillowcase. If we let her get started on *this* subject, especially with someone like Jack to pound it at, we'd be here like sitting ducks when the Twisters marched up.

"Will somebody please give me back my watch?" I said. "It belonged to my dad."

"His dad's dead," Gemma said.

"Oh, I'm so sorry," Trudy said. She had the watch now. I wasn't sure how she'd gotten it off Jack. "That must be such an awful thing. Was it cholera or diphtheria?"

"It was cancer," Michael said. "People don't die from cholera and diphtheria much in 1999. Not in the United States, anyway. We've got antibiotics."

"What are anti-whatever?" Jack asked.

I could see Michael gearing up to explain it, and I wanted to head him off at the pass.

"Look," I said. "We do have a problem here. In fact, we've got two, and if we don't solve them we're going to end up in really big trouble, so I suggest—"

I'd actually been hearing the noise the entire time I was talking, but I'd been trying to ignore it. I knew the Twisters were out there. I knew they were after us, and everybody else, one way or the other. The problem is that if I let myself think like that, I can't think of anything at all. But there was no mistaking it. The curtains on Trudy's bedroom windows were drawn tight, but I

73

knew the creaking and groaning of tree branches when I heard it. I knew the sound of wood being crushed under an unbearable weight even better.

Gemma and Michael and I looked at one another with apprehension.

''Do something,'' Michael said.

Gemma did something. She strode across the room to the window—or came as close to striding as she could in her new clothes—and snapped the curtains back.

Jack and Trudy didn't know what they were going to see. Gemma and Michael and I thought we were going to see a Twister. We all got a great big surprise.

In the tree outside Trudy Doverby's window sat a big black, mournful-looking gorilla that was trying desperately to stuff its mouth with leaves.

14

It was Trudy who said it first, although she and Jack were both thinking it.

"It's the missing link," she said. "Look. Mr. Charlton was right."

"I think it's some kind of big monkey," Jack said. "They've got pictures of those in the *National Geographic*."

"I think it's the missing link," Trudy said again.

I could see Michael's ears starting to spout fire and smoke. I now knew what my little brother the genius couldn't handle. He was a creature of technology. Take him away from twentieth-century science, and he started to lose it on a regular basis.

"There is *no such thing—*" he began now.

Gemma cut him off. "He doesn't look dangerous," she said. "Or maybe it's a she. Whatever it is, it looks hungry."

"It's eating leaves," I pointed out.

"It's also looking at us," Michael said. "Did they have tame gorillas in 1899?"

"Why tame?" I asked him.

"Because he's staring right back at us," Michael said. "Just like I told you. Just like he's used to it. And if he wasn't used to it, I don't think he'd do that."

"I see what you mean," Gemma said. "If all he knew was the wild, then all he'd know was that people shoot at him, because that's what Bernard Charlton probably does."

"He couldn't be from around here anyway," Michael said. "There aren't any gorillas in Marsdentown. I don't think there ever were any gorillas around here, even millions and millions of years ago."

"I think it's beautiful," Trudy said. "It has the saddest eyes."

It did have the saddest eyes. Trudy wasn't making that up. It didn't seem to like the leaves it was chewing on, either. It kept stuffing them back in its mouth, but it seemed to be on some kind of automatic pilot.

"Maybe it escaped from a zoo around here someplace," Michael said. "Or maybe there's a circus in town."

"There isn't any zoo in Marsdentown," Jack said. "There isn't any zoo any closer than New York. And I know there hasn't been any news that there's a monkey that's gotten out to go wandering around."

"The circus that comes here doesn't have anything like this, either," Trudy said. "I've been every summer of my life and I haven't seen one. Just little monkeys."

"The circus isn't due here for another three weeks anyway," Jack said.

"It must have come through the way we did," Michael said. "There're apes at the Behavioral Sciences Department at the state university. That's only maybe a couple of miles from our house. If the Twisters have had the warp open for awhile—if this didn't start today, I mean—all kinds of things could have come through before we ended up here. The way the dinosaurs did the first time."

Gemma was pacing around, still staring at the gorilla. "I wish we had something sweet," she said. "A cookie, maybe, or a piece of cake."

"I wish we had our pizza back," Michael said.

"What's a pizza?" Jack said. "Is that some kind of weapon?"

"I've got a piece of cake," Trudy said.

We all turned to look at her. She blushed bright red.

"My mother says it isn't good to have food in the bedrooms, and I'm sure she's right and I wouldn't do anything like this normally, but I was reading this afternoon and I was hungry—"

"Oh, fooey," Jack said.

Trudy went to the table next to her bed. She opened the drawer and pulled out an untouched piece of chocolate cake with chocolate icing, arranged very carefully in the center of a small china plate. I almost lunged at it.

"I never got a chance to eat any of it," she said. "As soon as I got it up here, my mother called, and then we had the three of you."

"We don't want to wreck the plate," Gemma said. "It looks nice. Do you have a handkerchief or something like that?"

Trudy got a handkerchief. It wasn't anything anybody

could mistake for "nice." It had once been blue, but it had faded. It had started to fray around the edges.

"I should have thrown that out months ago," Trudy said. "If you want something more respectable, I could—"

"This is perfect," Gemma assured her. "I want something you won't mind losing, and this ought to do it."

Gemma strode back to the window. The gorilla was still sitting in the tree out there, mournfully munching its leaves. Gemma tipped the piece of cake onto the handkerchief and handed both the handkerchief with the cake on it and the china plate to me.

"Hold this for a second," she said. "Give it to me when I ask for it."

I knew what Gemma was going to do, and as I watched, she proceeded to do it. First, she opened Trudy's window and leaned out, cooing softly at the gorilla. The gorilla seemed to be fascinated by her voice and not in the least interested in running away. Then Gemma started to ease herself out the window onto one of the branches that had grown close to the house. She kept getting tangled up in her petticoats.

"Oh, this idiot stuff," Gemma said, hopping back into the room and pulling up her dress. She untied the petticoats at her waist and began to pull them off. "No wonder women didn't get the vote until 1920. It took them that long to figure out how to move in their clothes. Here, Trudy, hold this. I can't do anything with it on."

Trudy took the petticoats, looking shocked. *"Gemma,"* she said.

Gemma twisted her dress high on her legs and tied

it awkwardly around her waist. "You can't climb trees when you've got all this stuff on," she said. She sat back down on the window ledge and swung her legs out onto the branch just outside. A moment later, she was crawling along it in the direction of the gorilla.

"You want the cake?" I asked her.

She turned to look at me. Then she leaned back into the house and took the handkerchief I was holding out. It was a good thing she did, because if she had gone much farther, she would have been out of reach. The gorilla looked at us both with faint interest, but no fear.

"The Behavioral Sciences Department at the university," Michael said positively. "No fear at all. Not even a whole lot of curiosity."

Gemma moved slowly along the branch, balancing herself carefully. When she got close enough to touch the gorilla, but not close enough to be pressed up next to it, she stopped and worked herself around until she was sitting down. The gorilla was definitely interested in Gemma, but it still didn't look scared.

"You okay?" I called out to her.

"I'm fine," she said. "Hi, little gorilla. Nice gorilla. Would you like a piece of cake?"

Gemma broke off a piece of cake in one hand and held it out. The gorilla looked it up and down and then reached for it. Its hand was twice the size of Gemma's. It made the piece of cake look like a dust mote.

"It likes it," Gemma said.

This was an understatement. The gorilla truly and sincerely loved that cake. As soon as it got it into its mouth, it came hopping across the branch at Gemma, looking for more.

Gemma handed over the handkerchief. "The poor

thing is starving," she said. "I wonder what it usually eats. It doesn't like the leaves we've got around here."

What the gorilla liked was the cake. It grabbed Gemma's yellow dress and began poking at it, making Gemma giggle.

"This *is* a tame gorilla," Gemma said. "You know what I think it's doing? I think it's looking for pockets."

"I think it's looking for cake," I said uneasily. "Gemma, listen. I don't think there is any such thing as a tame gorilla once the gorilla gets past a certain age. And this one looks full-grown. I think it's going to find out you don't have any more cake and then it's going to be upset."

"It's got a tag," Gemma said. "Let me read it. Then I'll come in."

Gemma leaned forward and reached for the tag around the gorilla's neck. Now that she had hold of it, I could see it, too. She was bending over to read it when I saw the scenery behind her start to tremble.

Michael realized what was happening before I did. He rushed at the window, frantic, waving his arms.

"Gemma," he shouted. "Gemma, get out of there. There's a Twister."

There was a Twister, too. If it had been any ordinary Twister, Gemma would have been dead. This, though, was the little one we had first seen on the other side of town—except that it wasn't as little as it had been. It must have grown three feet in the couple of hours since we'd seen it last. The only way I knew which one it was was by the little square bits of pizza crust still caught in its tentacles.

Instead of trying to kill somebody, the Twister grabbed the handkerchief with the cake crumbs on it out of the gorilla's hands and stuffed the whole mess into his mouth. Then it took off.

That was the point at which everybody panicked. The gorilla made a high-pitched noise and bolted into the branches of the real trees. Gemma shook and waved on her branch, finally got her balance and hurried crab-legged back inside. Jack Doverby kept hopping from one foot to the other.

"It's a tree," he kept saying. "It's a tree that walks."

Gemma threw herself down on Trudy Doverby's floor. "That's a gorilla used to people, all right," she said. "Do you know what the tag on that gorilla says? Pippi. *Pippi.* You remember Pippi. Pippi went missing from the Carlson Brothers Circus when it was parked not half a mile from my own house. In—"

"1997," I finished for her.

"Oh," Michael said. "I get it."

15

There are good parts and bad parts to being a boy genius. The bad parts all have to do with not having anyone around you can really talk to. The good parts have to do with being able to figure things out. Michael was sitting cross-legged on the floor, thinking furiously. When he thinks like that, it's almost as if I can see it.

"Hey, kid," I said. "Are you all right?"

"It's the sunspots," Michael said. "That's the point. It's the sunspots that are doing it."

"Doing what?" Jack said.

"We should have known when we first saw the gorilla," Michael said. "I mean, no European had ever seen a gorilla before 1869. I don't know when they started to have them here in zoos, but it probably wasn't as soon as that. It had to have come here from our time. That's the only way it makes sense."

"I still don't get it," I said. "I remember when Pippi

went missing from the circus. It was a big story. But that was two years ago. Are you saying that Pippi escaped from the circus and went wandering around for two years until she got caught in a plot by the Twisters?''

"Don't be silly," Michael said. "She never escaped from the circus. She just got caught in the warp. It's the sunspots. They do everything by vibrations, right? Well, sunspots affect vibrations in the air. They screw up radio and TV broadcasts all the time. Vibrations make sound waves and the waves get messed up by the sunspots and things get caught in the warp stream.''

"What's a warp stream?" Jack asked.

"It's the way the Twisters move through time. Time is a flow. One of my teachers told me that—''

"That sounds like a song," Gemma interrupted.

"Whatever. As an idea, it works. The time stream is getting all messed up because the Twisters are playing with it and they're being sloppy. They're not taking everything into account. And when they mess up, stuff gets caught, like this gorilla, or the dinosaurs that ended up in our basement, and then you've got a mess.''

Gemma had untied her dress and let it fall around her ankles again. "Michael, this is all very nice, but it isn't getting us anywhere. It isn't getting us home, for instance, which is where I want to go. And what about the Twisters? Every time we've seen them do something like this they've been—''

"Planning some kind of attack," I finished for her. "I know. I've been thinking about that a lot.''

"I've been thinking about it, too," Michael said. "I've been thinking that there's only one way to stop them.''

"How?" I asked.

Michael is usually all theory. I'm the one who's had to have most of the ideas on how to launch effective operations against the Twisters.

Michael was standing up. "We have to make a pizza," he pronounced solemnly.

I thought that this was it. The stress had finally gotten to him. He'd finally gone nuts. He wasn't thinking straight anymore.

"Michael," I said gently.

"Think," Michael said furiously. He knew I was patronizing him. He hates it when I do that. *"Think,"* he said again. "We can't get home unless we get back to the portal, right?"

"Right," I said.

"And the portal is right back where our house and Gemma's are going to be, so that's where we have to go."

"Right," I said again.

"And we should get Pippi back there, too," Michael said. "because if we leave her here she'll just die, with that Charlton man thinking she's the missing link and shooting at her—"

"Don't get started on the missing link," Gemma said.

"We, we ought to bring her back," Michael insisted. "So we've got that to think about. And then we've got the Twisters. We have to get the Twisters to follow us back there."

"You're nuts," Gemma told him.

Michael ignored her. Michael was ignoring everybody. "They've got to have the stuff downstairs to make a pizza," he said. "Bread dough, that's just flour and water and stuff. And oil—"

"They won't have olive oil," I said. "And they won't have mozzarella cheese, either."

"We can make an American pizza, just like Mom does when she works too late to want to cook. We can use regular oil and cheddar cheese and—they've got to have tomatoes. Do you have tomatoes?" he demanded of Trudy.

"Yes," Trudy said. "We do. A lot. My mother keeps a garden out back."

"Good. Let's go. Because I don't think we've got much time."

"But why are we making pizza?" I asked. "What are we going to do with it?"

"But *what's* a pizza?" Jack demanded.

"It's food," Gemma said impatiently. "Now shut *up*."

"We're going to get the baby Twister to follow us," Michael said. "And then the other Twisters will follow. At least I think they will. Because all creatures protect their young."

"We could use chocolate cake instead," Gemma said.

"Not and be sure," Michael told her. "We don't know if the baby Twister liked it. He ran away before we could tell. We know he likes pizza."

"So why don't we get cake and give it to Pippi and get us all back to the portal and leave the Twisters where they are? We did it when they came through the Jurassic period—"

"This isn't the Jurassic," Michael said bleakly. "This place is full of people. And if the Twisters decide to go on the rampage here—they're going to really trash the place."

16

Gemma told Mrs. Doverby that pizza was a specialty her mother made, and that she was homesick for it. That was how we got to make our pizza. It was a strange version of the stuff, at least to me, and I wasn't at all sure that it was going to work as an enticement to the baby twister. It's amazing how much changes in a hundred years. Mrs. Doverby had never heard of mozzarella cheese. In 1999, she could have gone down to the local Stop and Shop and picked up fourteen different brands of the stuff.

At least Mrs. Doverby wasn't close-minded about it. Gemma bustled around the kitchen, for the first time acting the way Mrs. Doverby really thought a girl should act. Mrs. Doverby beamed. Gemma suggested that Michael and I give her a hand. Mrs. Doverby went on beaming, but she reacted as if Gemma had just made nonsense sounds.

"Don't be silly," she said. "This isn't the kind of thing boys are good at."

Then she shooed us off into a corner of the kitchen by flapping both her hands. Michael looked bewildered.

"I don't get it," he said. "I like to cook. I'm good at cooking. Why can't I cook?"

"Boys don't cook," Jack said. "They just don't. That's all."

Trudy rolled her eyes toward the ceiling, exasperated. I didn't blame her.

"Well, I cook," Michael said positively, "and Gemma's father cooks at home, and Mr. Barnaby up the street cooks, and half the chefs on television are men, so I don't see—"

"Television?" Jack said.

I decided this had gone far enough. I've read books where time travelers encounter people from the past and everybody gets together and talks about all the changes that are going to happen by the end of the twentieth century. They always seem to be having fun doing it, but now that I was doing it, I wasn't having any fun at all. There was just too much to explain, and Jack was just too stubborn.

"Listen," I said. "The point here is that we end up with a pizza, and Gemma can get us that."

"You're a better cook than Gemma is," Michael said.

"Maybe I am, but we don't have to eat the pizza if we don't want to—"

"What makes you think the baby Twister will like it if we don't?" Michael asked.

"Maybe I'm just worried that the grown-up Twisters will like it, too," I said. "Maybe a little less-than-perfect cooking—"

"The grown-up Twisters have never had any pizza."
Michael sounded furious.

I sighed.

Over by the stove, Gemma was pulling something off
the two flat cookie sheets she'd used instead of a pizza
pan. She'd used them because Mrs. Doverby didn't have
a pizza pan, and because Mrs. Doverby would not listen
to the possibility that you could cook a pizza flat on an
oven rack without anything under it at all. That, she'd
told us seriously, would be unsanitary.

"Look what I've got," Gemma said now. "It's not
perfect, but I think it's going to be all right."

Michael and Trudy and Jack and I advanced on the
stove. Michael looked downright suspicious. I was a
little worried about all the substitutions Gemma had
made. She'd used ham instead of pepperoni. She'd had
to make the tomato sauce herself instead of getting it
out of a jar, and Mrs. Doverby didn't have basil or
oregano. I put food markets with mostly prepared food
in them up there with air conditioning among the things
I was going to be glad to get back to.

Gemma lifted the pizza carefully and brought it across
the room to the big kitchen table. She set it down on
the tablecloth and let us all look at it.

"The mushrooms look authentic enough," I said
cheerfully.

Michael gave me a withering look. "Lard instead of
olive oil," he said. "And that's just the beginning."

"I think what matters is how it tastes," Gemma said.

Mrs. Doverby was already advancing on us with a
great big knife. It was nothing like a pizza cutter, but
it looked sharp enough to slice through bone.

"Here we are," she said in a bright voice. "What

do we do with it now, Gemma? Do we eat it right away or do we wait for it to cool off?''

"I think we should eat some of it right away," Gemma said, "just to see how it came out."

"Fine," Mrs. Doverby said. "Fine. How do I cut this? Like a cake?"

"I can cut it if you want," Gemma said.

Mrs. Doverby handed Gemma the knife and stepped back. I was surprised for about half a second. Then I realized that Mrs. Doverby was trying to encourage a promising trend, the way my Mom does when Michael decides to clean his room without being asked. Cooking and being proud of your cooking was the sort of thing Mrs. Doverby thought girls ought to be interested in. From the expression on Trudy's face, though, I didn't think it was something Mrs. Doverby had had much luck getting her own daughter interested in.

I moved up to Mrs. Doverby's side, just to deflect any too-helpful comments she might make. The last thing we needed at this point was either Gemma or Michael going off on a lecture about How Boys and Girls Do Things in 1999. Mrs. Doverby didn't believe we came from 1999 anyway. Chief Doverby just thought that somebody—Bernard Charlton, probably, or maybe Harriet Winthorpe—had put us up to saying so.

"This is a beautiful house," I told Mrs. Doverby politely. "Could you tell me what street we're on?"

"Oh, we're not on a proper street," Mrs. Doverby said. "Town doesn't come out this far, although Henry says it will, sooner rather than later. It is a beautiful house, isn't it?"

"Yes," I said. "It is."

"They call the road out there Bellevue Place," Mrs.

Doverby went on. "Just like it was right in the middle of Paris, France. Can you believe that? That's the fault of old Mr. Davison's wife. He built the road, you see, when all that was out here was a farm he had, so he got to name it, and that fancy woman he brought down from Boston wanted Bellevue Place."

I knew Bellevue Place. In 1999, it was practically in the middle of town. There was no big Victorian house on it, though. I would have noticed a big Victorian among all those compact little Colonials.

"Hey, Michael," Gemma said. "Come over here. This is sort of—interesting."

I didn't know if "interesting" was what we were looking for, but I decided to check the pizza out anyway. Gemma had cut thin little slivers of it to hand around. She was trying to preserve as much pizza as possible for our maneuvers against the Twisters. I came over to the table and she handed me a piece.

"It's actually not bad," Michael told me. "I mean, if you didn't know what the real stuff tasted like, you could get to like this a lot."

"We went to England once," Gemma said, "and they had pizza like this there. With cheddar cheese and little kernels of corn on it."

"It's wonderful," Jack said.

I should have caught on sooner. Sometimes I can be so dense, I embarrass myself. If the Doverby house wasn't on Bellevue Place in 1999, something must have happened to it.

I was chewing on ham and a piece of green pepper when I heard the noise—a big thump that was followed almost immediately by a sucking, shaking sound. We all put down our pizza and looked at one another. Jack and Trudy and Mrs. Doverby were bewildered. Michael was scared to death.

The thump and the shaking were followed by another thump and even more shaking, but this time it was all much closer. It was right against the side of the house. I could feel the floorboards shudder under my feet.

"Jon," Michael said.

"Right," I said, as the thumping came again and the whole house began to shake. I thought the Twisters were going to tear the whole thing right out of the ground.

"Let's go," I said. "Everybody out of here. Now."

"But what is it?" Mrs. Doverby asked. "Is it an earthquake?"

We didn't have time to let her stand around and speculate. Gemma and Michael were already racing out of the house. Trudy was following them. I caught Jack's eye and nodded a little.

We got Mrs. Doverby through her own back door and into her own backyard just seconds before the first sounds of splintering came from the direction of the parlor.

17

It was like one of those stories we'd been reading in literature class, like an ancient myth from some country I'd never heard of. The sky outside was black, but not because it was choked by clouds. It was the Twisters out there, huge and moving, hemming us in from every side. I don't think we'd ever been so close to so many of them before, or so close to getting hurt, either. Even the first time, when some of them *had* hurt us, I'd felt like we were in more control than we were now.

To Jack and Trudy and Mrs. Doverby, the Twisters just looked like trees, gigantic evil trees that had come to life. As far as I could figure out, Mrs. Doverby had decided that these were trees and we were all in the middle of a terrible storm. One of the Twisters smashed a branch against the side of the house and broke a window. Mrs. Doverby hopped back and forth from foot to foot and clasped her hands.

"It's a twister," she called out to us, meaning a tornado. "We have to go into the cellar and wait it out."

I knew that the last thing we wanted to do was to go to a cellar. In a cellar, we'd be trapped. The Twisters would just love to have us trapped.

Michael ran up to me and nearly knocked me over. "I have the pizza," he shouted. "I have the pizza. We can do what we planned to do, and hopefully fast; this is hot."

Michael *did* have the pizza. He had it all sort of folded up in his hands. It was making a sticky mess of him. In the meantime, the Twisters were still working on the house. They were going to take it apart board by board.

"It's an earthquake," Mrs. Doverby said, crying now.

A big tentacle-branch came down on the house's roof and ripped off an entire row of shingles. Another tentacle branch pulled a block of siding off the house's side. If this had been a twentieth-century house, it would have been matchsticks already.

"Jon," Gemma shouted, coming up behind me. "Look. It's the baby. Hiding off there to the side."

"Right," I said, trying to think. It was hard to do, with all the noise. The Twisters weren't making any noise, but the house was. It was groaning and screeching. I could hear wood snapping, glass breaking, nails being pulled up by main force.

I turned to Gemma. "Take Michael and the pizza and see if you can get the little one to follow you. Head out to Bernard Charlton's place. Out to the warp."

"What are you going to do?"

"I'll be right behind you. I promise. There're just a

few things I've got to clear up. If I don't, we're all going to end up dead."

"That's the point, isn't it?" Gemma said. "That's what they want. We were wrong. They do recognize us. They want the three of us dead."

"Just go," I said.

Gemma gathered Michael and went, as fast as she could, in the direction of the road. I grabbed Trudy and spun her around.

"Go into the barn," I told her. "Grab your mother and go into the barn and don't come out until you don't hear any more noise."

"But what's happening?" Trudy asked. "What is this? What are those things?"

"Go," I said again.

Trudy went. The noise was getting worse and worse by the second. The house was coming apart at its foundations. By the time the Twisters got finished, there wasn't going to be anything left of it. If they had their way, there wasn't going to be anything left of us, either.

I ran up to Jack and shook him. He was just standing there in the middle of the yard, looking stunned. I was afraid he might be in shock.

"Get me an ax," I told him. "I need an ax. Do you have an ax anywhere around here?"

Jack took a second to snap out of it, but when he did, he was surprisingly calm. He was much more focused than I'd thought he'd be.

"An ax," he repeated. "That's good. They're trees. So we need an ax."

"Jack," I said.

"We've got axes all over the place," he said. Then he dashed into the barn, and for the worse second in my life I thought he had left me there. Then he dashed out again, carrying two long-handled axes, one in each hand.

"Don't want the short-handled ones," he said. "Don't want to get too close."

We were going to have to get very, very close, but I didn't mention it. Jack might be a little thick, the way I'd thought, but he was one of the bravest kids I'd ever seen. There were these enormous monsters, wrecking his house, breaking his windows, taking his porch and reducing it to shreds, and he just went right at them, as if they couldn't hurt him at all. I was a poor second on the scene. By the time I got there, Jack was already swinging.

We'd hurt a Twister before, but we'd never killed one. I had no idea what was going to happen if we wounded one badly. Jack swung his ax in a wide arc around his head and aimed right for the Twister's middle section, right for where Michael had always said he thought the Twisters' brains must be. Maybe Michael was right, too, because as soon as Jack's ax sank into the Twister's side, it fell to the ground and started to writhe. It also started to scream. I'd never heard a noise like that before in my life. I never want to hear a noise like that again.

"BWAAALEEEALG!"

The other Twisters turned to it right away. They stopped working on the house. They stopped paying attention to Jack or me. They just looked at the fallen one and began to prod it.

"Let's go," Jack hissed in my ear. "We've got to run. We've got to get out of here. They aren't going to stay like that for long."

18

For a moment, I thought Jack had forgotten Trudy and his mother waiting in that barn. The Twisters were circling around the one that lay on the ground. Some of them were wailing in the wind. Some of them were lashing out their tentacle-arms and causing damage to all kinds of things, including real trees. Jack ran around them and out toward the road. I kept expecting the Twisters to start ripping the barn to shreds.

I didn't like being all alone there in the backyard. The Twisters weren't paying any attention to me, but I thought they would, any minute now. I ran in the direction Jack had run and saw him up ahead of me on the road, heading in what I thought was the direction of town. I had to keep reminding myself that Marsdentown in 1899 was geographically the same place as Marsdentown in 1999. All the little things were so different, I kept getting confused. The Doverby house was on Bellevue Place. Bellevue Place was where the Historical Society was in the Marsdentown I was used to. That meant we were—right at the top of the hill that went down to the Methodist church, which was right on the road that led into town in one direction and out to my house— and Bernard Charlton's land—in the other. The light dawned just as I ran smack into Jack, nearly knocking him over. In all the confusion, I hadn't noticed him. He was standing stock-still, looking back at the terrible things that were the Twisters.

"What are those?" he demanded, grabbing me by the shirt.

"They're animals," I said, panting a little. "They come from another planet—"

"Don't make things *up.*"

"I'm not making things up," I said. "Look at them. They look like trees. But they feed. And they move. And they aren't rooted to the ground. And they bleed, Jack."

It was a stretch to call what the dead Twister was doing "bleeding." He was oozing something, but it didn't look like anything I'd ever called blood before.

"Look at them," I told Jack again.

Jack was looking at them, shaking his head. "We have to kill them," he said. "They're savage. They kill anything."

"You just killed the only one I ever saw killed," I said. "I can't say it can't be done because you did it, but look how many of them there are. And the ones we're looking at aren't the only ones."

"We'll find the rest of them. We'll kill them too."

"The rest of them are on the other side of a time warp," I told him. "They're on a different planet. Even Michael doesn't understand the technology and Michael understands more about science than anybody else I know.''

''We've got to get them out of here,'' Jack insisted.

''Yeah, well, we can do that,'' I said. ''If we can get them back to Bernard Charlton's place, we can at least get them out of Marsdentown in 1899. And once Michael and Gemma and I get back to 1999, we can close off the portal. At least temporarily. We've done it before.''

Jack stared at me long and hard. I knew he only half-believed all this stuff. I didn't blame him. I wouldn't have believed it at all if somebody had thrown it at me. Then he looked back at the Twisters. The one on the ground was dead. I was sure of that now. The Twisters surrounding it were starting to look restless.

''They're going to come after us any minute now,'' Jack said. ''We can let them chase us back to Mr. Charlton's place.''

''Maybe,'' I said. ''I don't know if it will work or not. That's why Gemma wanted to make the pizza. There's a baby one. We know it likes pizza. And we figured the big ones would want to protect their young, so if we could get the baby to follow the pizza, then we could get the big ones—''

I was babbling. Jack was not taking me seriously.

''Gemma can do anything she wants,'' he said, ''but we've got this.'' He swung the ax in the air. ''This will make them follow us.''

''Why?'' I asked stupidly. ''Do you think they want to fight with you? You'll get killed. They're bigger than you are and they're stronger than you are and they're faster than you are when they want to be—''

"They'll follow this because they can smell blood," Jack said.

That was when I became aware of the Twisters again, really aware of them. They'd been so completely concentrated on the one that was hurt, I'd almost stopped thinking of them as real. Now I saw that they had turned their attention back to us.

"Oh, rats," I said. "We're in trouble."

"We're going to run," Jack told me.

"We've got to do more than run," I said, although I felt a lot like running at the moment. "We've got to think of something smart—"

"They're big and they're clumsy. All we have to do is slow them down."

"But how?" I demanded.

The Twisters had begun to creep in our direction, very slowly, as if they didn't want to get us alarmed. I was alarmed. I was as alarmed as I ever wanted to be.

"Jack," I said.

"Run," Jack said.

I thought he was going to go on down Bellevue Place. It's where I would have gone, if I had been making the choice. Instead, he turned around a hundred and eighty degrees and headed into the trees that surrounded the Doverby property on three sides. The trees were thick there, too, and they were old. They grew close together on the ground and their trunks were massive. Jack leaped into a gap between two of them and called back for me to follow.

"Come on," he shouted. "Run!"

I ran. It was a brilliant idea. I wish I'd thought of it myself. I was ashamed of myself for thinking of Jack as thick. My Mom's always telling me I shouldn't be so quick to judge. My Dad used to tell me that, too, when he was still alive to tell me. I guess I don't always listen.

The thing about the trees was that they slowed the Twisters way down. I moved through the brush behind Jack as quickly as I could go without twisting an ankle. I could hear the Twisters behind us, slashing at trees and knocking them down. I couldn't hear anything that sounded like a house or a barn coming apart. That made me feel a little better.

I caught up to Jack and grabbed him by the sleeve. "This is a great idea, really great, but are you sure we're going in the right direction? We have to go to Bernard Charlton's property."

Jack looked at me pitifully. "You know," he said. "They may have all this stuff you talk about in 1999, but I'll tell you what they don't have. They don't have boys with a halfway decent sense of direction."

19

We were headed in the right direction, although it took me a while to see it. Jack had it half right. It isn't that there aren't kids in 1999 who know where they are. It's that I can't generally find my way out of a paper bag. It causes me trouble sometimes, but it's one of the traits I shared with my dad, so I don't mind so much. I was a little embarrassed anyway, considering how long it took me to figure out that I was just up on Baldwin Hill, where the new middle school was being built the last time I saw my own house.

Behind us, the Twisters were groaning and screaming and moving. Mostly, they were slashing at trees and trying to push over the obstacles Jack's intelligence had put in their way. After a while, Jack and I weren't even really running anymore. I had a stitch in my side, and we were both worried about breaking something, like our legs. Fortunately for us, though, the Twisters were tangled up good. They were going to stay that way until they figured out they didn't have to be. I was hoping that wouldn't be any time soon, but I knew it probably would be.

"You know," I told Jack, as we walked through the thick stand of trees, "that's not the kind of thinking they seem to be good at. What they're good at is these crazy machines—"

"Dump your ax," Jack said.

"What?"

"Dump your ax. Drop it. Just like I dropped mine about forty feet back."

It was true. Jack didn't have his ax. I looked at mine.

"We don't want them following us right up to getting us," Jack said patiently. "They're following the smell on the ax. Or they might be. So the ax is back there. When they find the ax, we'll be someplace else."

"Oh," I said.

"You ought to drop your ax," Jack said, "just in case you got some of their smell on it, because we don't want—"

"Right," I said. I dropped the ax. *Now* who was being thick?

Jack nodded with satisfaction. Then he turned around and started walking again, through the trees. Now that we were far enough away from the Twisters, the world seemed to be a fairly calm place. The sky over our heads was mostly blocked off by the dense leaf color, but where it came through, I could see that it was blue and clear. I'd forgotten what a great day it had been, back in 1999, when all this had started.

"Let me ask you something," Jack said. "Those things Gemma was telling Trudy, about women getting the vote when you come from. And boys cooking. Was that true?"

"Yeah," I said.

"Woo boy," Jack said.

Up ahead, I could see patches of light. The stand of trees was ending. I pointed and shrugged. Jack said, "That's the road. We're right up the hill from Charlton's place. It won't take us long to get down there."

"I don't hear much from the Twisters," I said. "Maybe they're still tangled up back there but good."

"Maybe they are. But they can't be completely stupid. They thought up this time warp thing to begin with. Unless you did."

"No," I said. "We didn't. We don't have time-warp technology yet in 1999."

Jack grunted. We had come to the end of the trees. We both stopped for a moment to listen to the Twisters, but their sounds were far away. I could still tell they were coming closer.

"They're headed for us," Jack said. "We'd better go before they catch up."

"Back through the warp," I told him.

He grunted again. Then we came out onto the road and I could look around at what would be the Bonaventure house one of these days, and a little mini subdivision of three raised ranches that would put the town zoning board into agony for months.

We crossed the road and started down the second part of the hill. Once we moved through the first stand of trees on the ridge, the ground was mostly clear. I wondered if Bernard Charlton had cleared it, or if somebody had used it for pasture.

We had just passed the place where a girl named Lisa

Corrigan would live a hundred years or so in the future, when we saw Michael and Gemma. They were both sitting cross-legged on the ground, looking completely relaxed. Michael was holding a piece of pizza in the air, looking as if he were examining it. Then the pizza seemed to float into the air by itself, and that was when both Jack and I saw it.

"That's one of those things," Jack said. "He's sitting right next to one of those things."

"They both are," I said.

They were both sitting next to Pippi the gorilla, too, but it wasn't the kind of detail I was noticing. I don't think Jack was, either. We both took off at a run. I think we were both panicking. I know I was scared to death.

We were all the way up to them, ready to do God only knew what to protect my best friend and my baby brother, when Gemma leaped to her feet and waved her arms in the air.

"Look," she said. "It *is* a baby. And it isn't dangerous at all. It loves us."

"It loves pizza," Michael said.

Michael took another piece of pizza out of his lap and tried to give it to Pippi. He ended up having to split it in half.

"It eats like an elephant," he said. "You wouldn't believe it. No wonder they get so big."

As far as I could tell, it had grown at least another foot since I'd seen it last.

"The poor thing is hungry," Gemma said, reaching out to pat its bark. The baby Twister squirmed and shivered under her hand. Then it did something that looked like it was trying to nuzzle her. Gemma kissed it.

"Good grief," I said.

"I think we'd better make up our minds what we're going to do next," Jack said. "I think they've figured out how to get to us."

I lifted my head and listened. Jack was right. The faint sounds of the Twisters fighting the forest were gone. What had replaced them was the low rumbling of Twisters on the march.

They were coming right at us.

20

should have known that it would happen quickly. I
should have known that Jack was wrong about the
Twisters following the smell of blood on the ax. As
far as Michael and Gemma and I knew, the Twisters
didn't even have a sense of smell. They hunted by
some kind of almost telepathic tracking instinct that
had always been the thing that frightened us most
about them.

I looked around at the three of us, standing exposed
in the clearing where we'd first been dumped into the
nineteenth century. We had to think of something and
think of it fast, but I didn't have the faintest idea what.

"What's the matter?" Jack asked.

Michael and I looked at each other. "We don't really
know what caused the warp," Michael said. "I mean,
they've got the technology that gets them from their
planet to earth—"

"We don't understand it, but we know it must exist," I put in.

"—but when they end up someplace like this, it's a mistake," Michael went on. "They don't want to be here. They want to be in 1999."

"How could they end up here by mistake?" Jack asked.

"They don't have enough technology," I said. "They're not really great at some things. Their physical makeup prevents them from mining metal, for instance, the way people can—"

"They want a time with cars and trucks and planes," Michael said. "They want it all done for them. So when they end up at an earlier time, it's always a mistake."

"And to get back to the time we started in," I said, "we have to figure out what the mistake was and how to use it. Only right now, we don't know what the mistake was."

"It was sunspots that time there were dinosaurs in the basement," Michael said. "But I don't think it was sunspots this time. I think—"

"We can't just stand here," Jack said. "They're going to be coming down here right about—"

"Now," Michael said.

I should have known the Twisters had arrived. Michael's face had gone as white as untouched snow. I turned around and there they were, up at the top of the ridge, a whole army of them. I don't think I'd ever seen so many of them stretched out together like that. My mind was suddenly full of crazy ideas about Shakespeare and this play we had read part of in class, where this entire forest advances on a castle. Except that in that case, it was soldiers dressed up to look like a forest, and I remember thinking at the time that the idea was really stupid. Now I wasn't so sure. It was impressive, watching trees march like that, even if their marching was kind of odd looking, because Twisters don't really move like soldiers.

I made myself snap out of it. Michael was counting on me, and my paralysis was scaring him to death. The Twisters were moving slowly—just in case we had more weapons, I think. There were only five or six of them, but they were so big it felt like more.

"Okay," I said, making my voice sound as take-charge and commanding as I could, for Michael's benefit. "This is what we're going to do—"

"Jon, look," Gemma shouted, running at us as fast as she could go. I was as grateful as anything, because I didn't really know what we ought to do. Then I looked up at the ridge and went cold. The Twisters were moving faster now, massing for attack.

"Look," Gemma said again, stopping in front of us. She held something in the air that I took a little while to identify. It was her thumb harp.

"For Pete's sake," I said. "We don't have time for—"

"Watch," Gemma commanded.

She stroked on the thumb harp's string. It gave out a tiny sound. Then the air around us began to ripple thickly, as if it were made of Vaseline.

"What happened?" I asked. "What was that?"

"Yes!" Michael shouted. "Yes! Yes! Yes! We've got it."

"Got *what?*" Jack asked.

"We caused the mistake," Michael said happily. "It was the harp. The harp makes sounds, don't you see?

Sounds cause vibrations. And if you throw vibrations at one another, they mess one another up."

"Different sounds make different waves," Gemma said. "It depends on what you do with the harp."

"Do something now," Jack said.

The Twisters were halfway down the hill. They had started to wave their tentacle-branches in the air. The world around us was beginning to look like it was in the middle of a storm again. A full-grown Twister is three or four times as tall as a baby Twister—as tall as a good-size tree. If you get enough Twisters together, they always manage to make it look as if they're blocking out the sun.

"Play another note," I told Gemma.

She played another note. The air rippled. I caught a glimpse of something that looked like a blizzard happening all around us. It was even cold, but it was over in a moment. We had to be right at the edge of the warp. And the sound vibrations Gemma was making were disturbing it.

"Wrong note," I said, trying to be calm.

The Twisters had caught the sound, or the vibration that caused the sound. They had slowed up again, probably confused by a vibration that wasn't of their own making and wasn't something they were used to, like a human voice. Their slowness was a relief, but it wasn't enough. Gemma played another note and we caught a glimpse of trees, more trees than I would have believed possible—our neighborhood, back when most of North America was a forest.

"What were you playing on that thing when all this started?" I asked her. "Do you remember that?"

"Oh," Gemma said. "I think it was—"

She started another note. The air rippled. I caught a glimpse of a house. Gemma's house.

"We've got to get out of the way," I said. "We can't be where your house is when we go back in time. We'll get killed."

"We've got to go back to the tree," Michael said.

"I wish we had an ax," Jack said. "They're still coming. We've got to do something about them."

They *were* still coming. The tree where Gemma's tree house would be was farther back into the clearing. Jack was in more and more danger every moment he stayed with us.

"Go back to your house," I told him. "Run as fast as you can. Make sure Trudy and your mother are okay."

"But I can't leave you here," Jack said. "It wouldn't be right."

"It'll be fine. We know how to get back through the warp. And once we get the vibrations started, they'll go too. They'll make use of the opening. They don't want to be here."

We'd been moving backward toward the right tree every moment we talked. Now Gemma twanged the thumb harp again. The air rippled again. One of the trees in front of us suddenly sprouted a ladder.

"We've got it," Gemma said.

Jack's mouth was hanging open wide enough to drive a truck through.

"Get out of here," I told him again. "That's the ladder to the tree house Gemma's mother built. We can go right back up it and into our own time."

"But—" Jack said.

It was Michael who convinced him. Michael wasn't waiting for anybody. He was up that ladder in no time at all, and as he went, he disappeared. He had to disappear. He was changing centuries.

"What the heck," Jack said.

"Go," I told him.

We both looked back up to the ridge together—but the army of Twisters was nowhere near the ridge anymore. It was at the bottom of the hill and just at the far side of the clearing. And it was picking up speed.

"Go," I said again.

This time, Jack went. He looked from me to Gemma to Pippi to the baby Twister, and then he went. I turned my back to him and trusted that he'd get away safely enough. The Twisters weren't after him. They were after us, and after a way to get back to their own place and time.

"Okay," I said to Gemma, "Let's move it."

She played the note on her thumb harp again. The air rippled again. The ladder appeared again, and this time it steadied.

"Play that note long and hold it," I told her.

Gemma did. The ladder was more than steady now. It looked solid.

"I don't know how long this is going to last," I told her. "We'd better use it while we can. Get moving."

"We've got to take them with us," Gemma said.

One of the "us" Gemma wanted to take was Pippi—but that was the easy part. Pippi had seen the ladder. She was already on her way up it. The other of the "them" was the baby Twister, which Gemma seemed determined to keep for a pet.

"You've got to be nuts," I said.

"It's a baby," Gemma said furiously. "Just look at

111

it. It's scared to death. We can't leave it here for those—those things—"

"We're not going to leave anything here," I said. "And those things are its family. What would we do with it? Keep it in your garage?"

"But—"

"And they'd come after it," I said. "Is that what you want? They'd come after it just the way you'd come after a child of your own if the circumstances were similar. And you know it."

"But *Jon*—"

"We're losing the ladder," I said.

The air around us was rippling again. The ladder was beginning to look like smoke. We weren't losing the Twisters, though. They were moving faster now. They were much more sure of themselves, and they were nearly on top of us.

I pushed Gemma toward the ladder and watched her grab hold. Then I grabbed hold myself and started to climb up behind her. The baby Twister sat on the ground near our tree, unable to climb anything at all. If it had been human, I would have said it looked ready to cry.

I almost messed myself up. I almost started thinking of it the way I think of Michael, and if I'd done that I would have had to save it. Then one of the adult Twisters ran right up under the ladder and snaked out a tentacle in my direction. I was up those rungs in a shot. But the Twisters were right behind me, right in the warp. And I knew that I had to move fast. Because we had to pull them through—but not through to us.

Forcing myself through to 1999 felt a little like forcing myself through rubber. It felt harder than it had going in the other direction. I stumbled sideways and hit something hard. It turned out to be the packing crate we'd been using as a table to hold the pizza. I steadied myself and looked around. I was in the tree house Gemma's mother had built. Gemma was sitting cross-legged on the floor, looking ridiculous in her yellow dress. Michael looked even more ridiculous in his knickers.

And right in the middle of everything was a tentacle-branch, waving through the warp.

"Just a minute," Michael said. He grabbed the thumb harp out of Gemma's hand and twanged it mercilessly. The air went wild again—patterned and thick. And then the oddest thing happened. For a moment, we were all up in the air—Gemma and Michael and me, Pippi and the baby Twister and the big Twisters. It was as if we were all suspended in space and time. Then time seemed to snap, like a rubber band pulled too tight—and it was 1999 again, with no Twisters in sight.

"Where do you suppose they are?" I asked. "Back in 1899?"

Michael shrugged. "I don't think so. We seem to have moved them. They're not here."

"And Marsdentown is still here," Gemma said. "So they never destroyed it."

I looked up to see Pippi disappearing into the woods. That was going to be interesting, too—but I decided not to bring it up. Somebody would run across Pippi today, and panic, and she'd finally get picked up and returned to the circus that was her home.

Gemma was up and pacing. "I was looking at these clothes," she said. "Do you think they'll believe us if we told them what happened and we showed them these clothes?"

"Your father would tell us we had great imaginations

and that I'm going to grow up to be a dynamite science-fiction writer someday,'' I said. ''Our mothers would just figure you found some stuff to dress up in.''

''That's what I thought too,'' Gemma said. She lay back and looked up into the leaves. ''I wish we hadn't had to leave the baby behind,'' she said. ''They'll only teach it to be evil, just like them. We could have turned it into our friend.''

The idea of having a Twister as a friend did not exactly appeal to me, but I let it go. I wanted to go home and take a bath and get Michael into some sane clothes. I wanted—

''I want something to eat,'' Michael said. ''I never got much of anything all day. I'm starving.''

Gemma and I had the same thought at the same moment.

''As long as it isn't pizza!'' we said.

21

One Saturday morning three weeks later, just after the start of school, Gemma climbed our front porch, knocked on our door and asked my mother if Michael and I had anything to do with our day. The formal invitation was a little strange, since Gemma's mom and mine are best friends, and Gemma's in and out of our house all the time, but there she was. Michael and I didn't have anything to do with the day, as a matter of fact. Michael had been up since six playing with his computer. I was trying to sleep in.

Gemma waited in our living room while Michael finished what he was doing and I got dressed. From where I was standing in the bathroom brushing my teeth, I could hear her discussing the amazing recovery of Pippi the gorilla in Marsdentown's Hanover Park with my mom. It *had* been an amazing discovery, too. Hanover Park has swings, and Pippi had apparently decided that she really loved them. She was swinging away when a young mother and her two toddlers showed up to play in the park. The young mother had a screaming fit. Pippi just went on swinging.

"It's a good thing she was so used to people," my mother was saying. "I mean, really. Losing your head like that, when you have children with you. If Pippi had been dangerous, they'd all be dead."

"Mmmm," Gemma said.

I decided my teeth were as white as they were going to get. I went down the hall and poked my head into Michael's room.

"Let's go," I said. "Gemma's waiting."

"I'm finished," Michael told me.

I didn't ask Michael what he had finished with. I wasn't sure I would have understood it anyway. I waited for him to get up and come into the hall. Then I let him go downstairs in front of me. Gemma was still sitting on our couch, looking polite. To grown-ups, Gemma *always* looks polite.

"Oh, there you are," my mother said. "I'm glad you're getting out. I was afraid Michael was going to spend the whole weekend with that computer."

"We're going to walk into town, if you don't mind," Gemma said.

My mother didn't mind. She was having one of her crazy days about the house, which meant that she wanted to spend her Saturday cleaning up after our cleaning lady. She would be happy to have Michael and me out of the way. I knew from experience that I would be more than happy to be out of the way.

"Have a good time," Mom said.

The next thing I knew, we were all out on our porch.

"You want to go sit in the tree house?" I asked. "It's warm enough."

"I want to go into town," Gemma said. "There's something I've got to show you. Guess what the creative writing club did yesterday?"

The creative writing club was new with Gemma this year. She used to say she would never want to be a writer like her Dad. The business was too crazy. Now she was busy writing short stories and underlining things in other people's novels. Isaac Asimov had been both a scientist and a writer, she kept telling me. So there was no reason she couldn't do it, too.

"Where could the creative writing club go?" I asked her. "Do we have a publishing house around here I don't know about? Did you go to the newspaper?"

"We went to the Historical Society," Gemma said.

"Why?" Michael asked her.

"We were learning about research," Gemma said. "How to do it and places you could go to find information. So we went to the Historical Society. And there's something you've got to see."

"Maybe," I said cautiously.

Actually, after we'd gotten back from the nineteenth century, I'd done some research of my own. I'd gone looking for the Doverby house, and when I couldn't find it—my recollections that day had been absolutely correct; Bellevue Place was a little subdivision of raised ranches and tiny colonials in 1999—I'd gone to City Hall to find out what had happened to it. When the old guy in the records department told me that the house had been wrecked by a "twister," I nearly jumped out of my skin—but he was only talking about a tornado. That was how the Great Twister Invasion was written up in Marsdentown history, as the Summer of the Tornadoes.

We were up at the top of the hill and passing the Methodist church. City Hall was right in front of us across the green. To our right was the small colonial house that had been turned into the Historical Society.

"I hope this is something good," I said. "Because if it's about the Doverby house, I already know—"

"I know you already know," Gemma said. "It's not about the Doverby house. It's about Marsdentown's most famous citizen ever. You've got to see."

Gemma was so eager to get where she was going, she was half running. Now she decided to run and get it over with, and I had to pump like crazy to keep up with her. Michael must have been restless, too, because he took off as fast as he could go. He ended up waiting for us on the Historical Society steps.

There was an old lady sitting at a desk just inside the door. She had very white hair and wore a blue cardigan sweater in spite of the heat. Gemma nodded to her politely. She looked suspiciously at both Michael and me. We followed Gemma through the front room and into a little back hall.

"It's right here," Gemma said, going through a door at the very back. "When I saw it I just about died."

There was a sign hanging over one of the display cases at the back of the room that said: MARSDEN-TOWN'S FAMOUS DAUGHTER. Gemma grabbed me by the sleeve and pulled me over, although I wasn't much interested. I knew all about Marsdentown's Famous Daughter. Everybody did. They told you all about her in school.

I looked down at an old sepia-lined photograph of a

woman in a flight jacket and off-white trousers standing next to a primitive prop plane: Gertrude Sayle, one of the great pioneers of the early days of flight and the only woman to earn that distinction. Our teachers always called her "Marsdentown's Own Amelia Earhart."

I turned away from the picture, a little annoyed—and then I stopped and turned back.

"Looks familiar, doesn't she?" Gemma said. "Read the caption."

I read the caption. It said: **Mrs. Gertrude Sayle, born Gertrude Doverby—**

"Oh, boy," Michael said.

"That's Trudy," Gemma said triumphantly. "Trudy is short for Gertrude. Do you think that would have happened without us? Do you think we caused that?"

"I think Trudy was well on her way to doing something spectacular before we ever showed up," I said. "Maybe we just, you know, gave her a little hope to hold on to."

"Well, I'll show you something that wouldn't have happened without us," Gemma said.

She pulled me over to the display case on the west wall and pointed at another photograph. This was the picture of a political rally, one of those old-fashioned ones where people carried flags and waved signs. The caption read: **Marsdentown turns out to greet its first homegrown U.S. senator.**

"Gemma," I said, "that definitely would have happened without us. What could we possibly have to do with—"

"Look at the picture again," Gemma said. "Look at the senator."

I looked. It took me a while to make it out, because

he had changed a lot as he'd grown older—but I couldn't help seeing who it was. Michael saw it, too.

"Jon," Michael said. "That's—that's—"

"That's Jack Doverby," Gemma said triumphantly. "And it's not just that he became a U.S. Senator. Read the rest of the caption."

I did. It said: **Senator John Doverby was elected to the U.S. Senate on a platform that promised his vote in favor of an amendment to the Constitution that would extend the right to vote to women.**

"Jack did that?" I asked, almost stupefied.

Gemma crowed. "If you think that's not changing anything important," she said, "I think you're nuts."

They're super-smart, they're super-cool, and they're *aliens*!
Their job on our planet? To try and resuce the...

RU1:2 **GONERS**
79729-1/$3.99 US/$4.99 Can

One day, Xela, Arms Akimbo, Rubidoux, and Gogol discover a
wormhole leading to Planet RU1:2 (better known to its inhabitants
as "Earth") where long ago, all 175 members of a secret diplomatic
mission disappeared. The mission specialists scattered through time
all over the planet. They're Goners—and it's up to four galactic
travelers to find them.

THE HUNT IS ON
79730-5/$3.99 US/$4.99 Can

The space travelers have located a Goner. He lives in Virginia in
1775 and goes by the name "Thomas Jefferson." Can they convince
the revolutionary Goner to return to their home planet with them?

ALL HANDS ON DECK
79732-1/$3.99 US/$4.99 Can

In a port of the Canary Islands in 1492, the space travelers find
themselves aboard something called the *Santa Maria*, with Arms
pressed into service as a cabin boy.

SPITTING IMAGE
79733-X/$3.99 US/$4.99 Can

RABID TRANSIT
79734-8/$3.99 US/$4.99 Can